THEIR FATAL SECRETS

A gripping crime mystery full of stunning twists

JANICE FROST

Published 2017 by Joffe Books, London.

www.joffebooks.com

This book is a work of fiction. Names, characters, businesses, organizations, places and events are either the product of the author's imagination or are used fictitiously. Any resemblance to actual persons, living or dead, events or locales is entirely coincidental. The spelling is British English.

ISBN-13: 978-1-912106-16-5

To my loyal readers.

Prologue

For the past three hours, Josh Connors and Logan Price had been in one of the bars down by the marina, playing drinking games with a bunch of their friends from uni. There had been two 'boat races' involving Josh downing two pints in record time accompanied by loud, raucous singing. Now, he and Logan were walking back to their accommodation, arguing about which of them was more wasted.

At the bridge over the River Strom, Josh came to a swaying halt. "Oh, man, I really gotta puke." He leaned over the wall and heaved. Numerous beers and Josh's dinner splashed into the river below.

"Oh, gross," Logan slurred. "Hey, I need to take a piss."

Josh didn't hear him.

"Wassat?" His finger wavered in the direction of a dark shape bobbing in the water a couple of metres away.

Logan squinted. "Dunno. Dead dog?"

"Too big."

"Big dead dog?"

Josh gripped his arm. "Shit, Logan. I think it's a body."

Logan gave an edgy laugh. "Yeah, right. It's a bloody dog or a shopping trolley or something that's been dumped in the river." While he spoke, a lorry lumbered over the bridge above them, and its lights briefly caught the floating shape. It was a sobering sight.

"Josh! What the fuck?"

Josh had clambered onto the wall. He sat with his legs dangling over the edge, arms raised in a diving position.

"You're too pissed to swim, mate!" cried Logan.

There was a plop, and Josh entered the water.

"Jeez!" Logan fumbled clumsily with his phone. It took three attempts to get it right, but somehow he got through to the emergency services and gabbled out a message. The woman on the other end was still talking when Logan lost the call.

It was too dark to see much in the water. Remembering that there was a torch on his phone, Logan managed to activate it. He directed the beam at the spot where he could hear Josh splashing around.

Josh had reached the inert, bobbing shape and was struggling to turn it over. Slowly the body rotated face up.

A scream of pure horror pierced the night air, causing Logan to stagger backwards. Down in the river, Josh's arms flailed wildly and his head disappeared under the water.

"Josh! Mate! What's going on?" Logan could see that his friend was struggling to keep afloat. Josh's head went under again. He resurfaced, swearing.

Josh trod water for a few moments, and then began swimming away from the body. After a few strokes he seemed to change his mind and swam back to embrace it in classic life-saving style.

"Josh! Are you okay?"

When he saw what Josh was dragging towards him, Logan's phone fell from his hand and landed in the river.

Everything went dark again, but Logan didn't mind. He'd already seen too much. Dead eyes staring out of a pulped face, a tangled mass of hair trailing in the water. He would see that face in his nightmares for years to come.

It seemed to take forever for Josh to reach the riverside with his ghoulish burden. Between the two of them they managed to haul her — for it was, or had once been, a woman — over the wall and onto the path. Immediately Josh covered her swollen mouth with his own in a heroic, if useless, gesture.

"What are you doing, mate?" Logan stood by, shifting from foot to foot. "There's nothing you can do for her." After a while Josh stopped and rolled away from the woman, exhausted.

"Close her eyes," Logan said.

"You close them." Josh's teeth chattered and he was shivering in great spasms. His hair was plastered to his head, and speckled with vomit. He heaved and spat onto the grass verge. "You called 999, right?"

Before Logan could answer, a police car pulled up near the bridge and a couple of uniformed officers hurried towards them. A moment later, an ambulance arrived and disgorged two green-suited paramedics. "Your services won't be needed, I'm afraid" one of the policemen said quietly.

One of the paramedics bent over the dead woman and confirmed what everyone already knew. Finally someone closed her eyes.

Chapter One

When Ava walked into the office, a helium birthday balloon weighted down with a giant envelope, was waiting on her desk.

DC Polly 'PJ' Jenkins rushed over and hugged Ava. "Happy Birthday!"

She held out a beautifully wrapped gift.

"Thanks, Peej. Hey! Where is everyone?" The room was eerily empty.

"Surprise!" Suddenly they jumped out from under desks and behind filing cabinets. Her colleagues blew whistles and cheered, and belted out an out of tune rendition of 'Happy Birthday.' Ava was touched.

"Thanks, guys. Cake's on me." She flourished a cake tin and pointed to the kitchen. They all trooped in after her. Within a couple of minutes, very little remained on the plate.

"Oops. Inspector Neal said if there was cake to save a piece for him." PJ looked at her own half-eaten slice. Ava wrapped what was left in a napkin and set it aside, wondering where Neal was. She opened PJ's gift. It was a pretty silk scarf in shades of pink and pale green.

"Wow! That's gorgeous. Thanks, Peej."

"We had a whip round and got you this." It was Dan from forensics. Ava eyed the package with suspicion. "It's not something disgusting from the lab, is it?" She remembered her first birthday on the force, when she'd peeled away multiple layers of wrapping paper to discover a jelly eyeball.

This gave rise to howls of affront.

"Okay! Okay!" Ava laughed. Moments later she was looking at a pretty silver necklace. She gasped with pleasure and held it up, twined around her fingers.

"Hey, you guys! I love it! I'll wear it this evening. First round's on me. Eight thirty at the Duke."

Noisy cheers greeted her offer, and fell away. A sudden hush descended on the room.

DI Jim Neal hovered in the doorway. "Many happy returns, Ava."

"We saved you a piece of cake, sir," PJ said. Ava held it out. The others quietly dispersed and returned to work.

"DC Jenkins, DS Merry, briefing room in five," Neal said, and retreated.

Ava and PJ gathered up their things.

"What's going on?" Ava asked.

"We've got a Jane Doe. A couple of students found her at two this morning. She was floating in the Strom under the bridge out past the marina. Chief's been up all night. Briefing's at nine thirty."

Ava had taken the previous day off, treating herself to an indulgent pre-birthday spa treat. She couldn't help a feeling of slight disappointment that she'd not been called out to attend the scene.

"I only just heard this morning," PJ said. "The DI was called out because he was the only senior officer available, given our current vacancy." PJ was referring to the DI post vacated by their former colleague, DI Reg Saunders. Saunders was currently experiencing the criminal justice system from the other side of the fence, having been charged with murder.

"DI Neal probably didn't want to spoil your birthday by calling you out in the middle of the night."

"Who accompanied him to the scene?" Ava asked.

"DS Knight."

Ava nodded. Tom Knight was an acting DS who'd transferred recently from Hertfordshire. He had previously worked with Reg Saunders, and she hoped the experience hadn't done him any harm.

Neal appeared and stood looking from PJ to Ava. "You've heard about our Jane Doe, then?"

Ava nodded. "Yes, sir."

Neal beckoned to them, and strode away along the corridor towards the briefing room. *For a man who's been up all night, he looks remarkably fresh*, Ava thought. Five o'clock shadow excepted, he might have come straight from a good night's sleep and a hot shower.

There was a lively atmosphere in the briefing room. Murder investigations typically started with a buzz that soon flat-lined in the daily grind of procedure. DSI George Lowe was present, but gave Neal centre stage. Around him the officers sat on chairs, perched on desks or simply stood, expectant.

Neal cleared his throat. "First off, we now know the identity of our Jane Doe. HOLMES came up with a positive match for her prints. Her name is Leanne Jackson. White female, twenty-three years old. Priors for public disorder and possession of controlled substances." He tapped the whiteboard behind him and a photograph of a young, dark-haired woman appeared.

"This was taken three years ago. It's the most recent image we have at the present time." Neal waited. Ava knew he was allowing time for people to jot down the name, write a brief description, become familiar with their victim. As soon as she was named, this woman became a real person, someone with family, friends, loved ones. Just like all of them.

Neal scanned the room. "A couple of students who'd been drinking in a club on the waterfront spotted Leanne's body in the River Strom at around two in the morning. One of them apparently needed to vomit and while acquainting the Strom with the contents of his stomach, got a sobering surprise."

Neal glanced briefly at the picture of the woman on the whiteboard. "The vomiting student," (no one laughed), "decided to play the hero and jumped into the river, even though the body was floating face down in the water. Leanne Jackson was beyond saving. Our young hero, Josh Lewis, managed to tow Leanne to the riverside where his friend, Logan Curry, helped him to heave her body over the wall and onto the path. Logan had already called 999 so by the time they laid Leanne's body on the path, the ambulance had arrived. The paramedics pronounced Leanne dead at the scene."

The room was silent. Ava could feel the unasked questions squeezing out the air. But Neal wasn't ready to take questions yet.

"Statements were taken from the students. It was noted that they were intoxicated and could not therefore be regarded as reliable witnesses. Not that they had witnessed anything more than a floating body. Josh's heroic rescue has probably done more harm than good in terms of forensics, but no one can blame him for acting as he did." Neal paused, as if expecting a challenge to his words. "As far as witnesses are concerned, so far we have none."

"Did she drown, sir?" someone asked.

"Too soon to say. She'd been severely beaten, but we won't know until after the PM if she was alive when she went into the water. Our press liaison officer has informed the local radio station and an appeal will go out this morning asking people to come forward if they saw

Leanne anywhere near the marina last night. Or if they witnessed anything suspicious. Some of you will obviously be doing a lot of legwork, questioning staff in venues around the marina, pubs, restaurants, cinema etcetera. We also need to get our hands on the CCTV footage for these venues, as well as any cameras along the riverfront. We will need to contact and question the owners of any boats moored at the marina." He looked around at them. "We're going to be busy, people."

"Will a diving team be searching the river?" Ava asked.

"Yes. That's already underway." Neal's phone rang. "Excuse me, it's Dr Hunt."

A low hum of conversation filled the room while he took the call. Ava watched Neal's face, trying to work out what Ashley Hunt was telling him. He looked weary now, his eyes red from lack of sleep. He stroked the stubble on his chin as though he'd just realised he hadn't shaved.

Neal suddenly looked straight at Ava. It was only for a moment, but it left her feeling exposed. Ava wasn't sure she wanted Neal to know that she was concerned, that she cared for him. Her feelings about Jim Neal were complex and she treated them like the symptoms of a potentially serious illness — ignoring them and hoping they'd go away. She suspected he did the same. Next to her, PJ gave her a dig.

"Ouch! What was that for?"

"You've got feelings for him, haven't you?" PJ whispered.

"Absolutely not."

"Fibber."

Neal ended his call and cleared his throat. The room fell silent.

"Dr Hunt has just confirmed that cause of death was drowning. It looks like Leanne was beaten, then tossed into the river. Her injuries would have prevented her from saving herself."

All eyes went to the image of the young woman on the screen. She was pretty, Ava thought. Pretty girls attracted attention. But there would be nothing pretty about Leanne Jackson now. Ava had seen bodies fished out of the water before. Their eyes were swollen, their bodies streaked with purple-pink patches of lividity, giving them the appearance of an unevenly cooked sausage.

Next, Neal assigned tasks to the various members of the team. There was much to allocate. Many of the mundane tasks, such as knocking on doors and taking statements were assigned to the PCs. They were routine jobs, but no one in the room underestimated their importance. A chance word from someone who had seen Leanne, or a conversation overheard between her and another party, might eventually lead to a successful conviction.

The team would try and build up a picture of the victim and her life — her health (including her mental health), social activities, education and work, her daily habits and routines, financial situation, and Internet history, all could help reveal why she ended up in the Strom.

The officers dispersed to go about their grim business, and the room emptied. Only Neal, Ava and Tom Knight remained.

"DS Knight's going to be working this one with us, Ava," Neal said. "You two know each other by sight at least, right?" They both nodded. "Tom, I'd like you to notify the next of kin. Take DC Jenkins with you. She needs the experience. Be compassionate, but find out what you can about Leanne's background and where she was in the past few weeks. Ask about friends, boyfriends, anyone she's been seen with recently. You know the drill. I want a complete picture of who this young woman was."

Tom nodded. "Yes, sir. Pleasure to be working with you, and you too, DS Merry." Tom Knight came from an East End council estate with a diverse ethnic population and his accent was 'Multicultural London.' Ava suspected that he toned it down now he was in the north, much as Neal moderated his Scots intonation.

"Same here," Ava said. Neal was right. She and Tom did have a passing acquaintance. Once, at a staff do, she'd seen him looking at her with more than a little interest, but Ava was used to men's looks.

"DS Merry, you and I are going out to the scene in five minutes."

"Ok, boss."

When they met in the car park, Neal's hair was damp at the edges. He'd evidently splashed his face with water to waken up. It wasn't that long since he'd left the scene.

Ava parked near the riverside, and she and Neal walked to the spot where Leanne's body had been found. Leanne wasn't the first nor would she be the last to be fished out of the Strom. Drunken revellers, students, party-goers, and stag-nighters had all ended up in the water over the years. Not to forget the despairing souls who jumped off the bridge in a bid to end it all.

A small crowd had assembled on the bridge to watch the proceedings on the path below. A couple of uniformed officers were ensuring that they didn't encroach on the scene. A representative from the local news station was there too. Ava recognised the reporter, standing with her back to the bridge, one of those big fluffy microphones hovering in front of her like a giant, hairy caterpillar.

A CSI crew had been working through the night, processing the immediate area. A diver sat in a yellow dinghy, and four other members of the underwater search team stood on the riverside, holding cables connecting them to the divers beneath the surface.

Much as she loved swimming and the occasional scuba-diving experience, the idea of groping her way around in the silt and filth of a murky riverbed in zero visibility brought out the claustrophobic in Ava. She looked at the spot where the yellow cables entered the water, picturing the divers beneath the surface searching in wide arcs, combing every inch of the riverbed with their fingertips, raking up all the detritus that ended up discarded there. She shuddered. The river was essentially a dumping ground. Its sun-dappled surface concealed just about anything you could imagine in terms of rubbish — used syringes, rusting tins and broken bottles . . . Was it possible to find a murder weapon among all that?

"Anything?" Neal asked one of the team, who had introduced himself as Paul Wells.

"Nothing so far, sir. All the usual crap, of course. We've been told we're looking for a blunt instrument of some kind? The girl had her skull crushed in as well as being beaten." Ashley Hunt, the pathologist, had been surprised that Leanne was conscious at all when she entered the water, given that she had extensive injuries as well as that crushing final blow to the head.

Neal nodded. "Aye, that's right."

Paul pointed. "We'll extend the search to the start of the marina. There's a shoreline search already underway, isn't there?" Neal nodded again. It was true that the murder weapon was often found near the scene of the crime, usually because killers panicked and wanted to get rid of it immediately. Unless it was a crime that had been meticulously planned. In a case such as this, it was anyone's guess whether they'd find a weapon.

Paul shook his head. "If you ask me, this is a stupid place to dump a body, right in the middle of town where it's going to be spotted so quickly. Not the cleverest move, but let's face it, killers haven't always got a lot upstairs."

"Maybe they had an argument, he killed her and then panicked," said Ava. "We know people's minds often go blank when that happens. They literally act without thinking. I'm amazed no one saw it happen. I know it was late, but the killer must have caught an incredibly lucky break to escape being seen, given all the bars along the marina."

"Maybe the killer didn't throw her in the river," Neal said. "Maybe he thought she was dead and was planning to dispose of her body elsewhere."

Ava looked at him. "You think she was on a boat?"

"It's a possibility."

Paul held up his hand. "Hang about. Lee's tugging on the line."

A couple of moments later the head and shoulders of a man wearing goggles and breathing apparatus broke the surface. With his back to the onlookers, he handed something to one of his colleagues in the dinghy, then turned and gave Paul a thumbs up.

Ava glanced at Neal. "Looks like we might have a murder weapon."

"Aye, maybe." Neal scowled at the bystanders on the bridge, and then turned away.

Dan Cardew of the forensics team held up the recovered object, encased in an evidence bag.

"It's an old-style flat iron. Traditional roses canal art design. My mum's got one. She uses it as a doorstop, but it's the sort of thing you might find on a narrowboat. A lot of people go for vintage stuff on those things. Like to create an olde world feel. Not that I'm an expert. Not been in there long, by the look of it."

"Can we get prints off it?" asked Ava.

"Possibly," he answered, surprising them all. "DNA too, if we're lucky."

"If it is our weapon, it makes it more likely that Leanne was on a boat and tried to swim to safety," Ava pointed out. "A flat iron's not the sort of thing you'd carry around in your pocket or pick up at the side of the road."

Dan took another look at the iron. "The design on this one is quite nice. It might be possible to trace the artist."

Neal nodded and gave a tired sigh. He turned to Ava. "Right, no point in us hanging around here any longer. I said we'd see Ashley when we're finished here."

With a brief wave at Dan, Ava ran after Neal.

* * *

Ashley looked as weary as Neal. Ava showed him a picture of the flat iron that Dan had forwarded to her.

He nodded. "Could be what caused the crack in her skull. A slantwise blow on the head from the flat side of an object like that could certainly have caused the kind of indent we see here." He showed them a picture of the woman's head and pointed to one side, just below her hairline. "Besides her other injuries, she also has a broken ulna, and substantial bruising to the other forearm."

These were classic defensive wounds. Leanne Jackson had been fending off blows to her head.

"So she drowned?" Neal asked.

Ashley nodded. "There was water in her lungs. She was alive when she entered the water. I'm thinking she might have lost consciousness for a while, regaining it before or as she hit the water. With her injuries, it would have been practically impossible for her to swim."

"We are thinking she might have jumped from a boat," said Neal.

Ashley nodded slowly. "That would work."

Ava brightened. "There can't have been too many boats passing along that stretch of the river at that time of night. Someone's bound to have seen something. And if not, it should be easy to spot a fifty-foot barge on the CCTV footage."

Neal frowned. "Yes, well let's not think this is going to be as straightforward as all that. It wouldn't take long to disguise the boat. It would only require a coat of paint."

He turned to Ashley. "Thanks, Ash."

Chapter Two

Jess Stokes stood among the throng of people on the bridge watching the police divers begin their trawl of the riverbed. She had been listening to the local radio station, Strom FM, when the news came through that a couple of students had pulled the body of a young woman from the river in the early hours of the morning. A later update had given the young woman's name as Leanne Jackson, causing a shiver to run down Jess's spine.

She hadn't thought about Leanne for a long time. They had never really been friends, but once Leanne had been there for her, and that wasn't something you forgot in a hurry.

Jess felt impelled to see the spot where Leanne had died. She hadn't meant to stay, but like the others around her, she'd been swept up by the buzz of activity on the riverfront and lingered to see what the divers might find. She was still there when DS Ava Merry arrived at the scene, accompanied by a man who was clearly in charge of proceedings. Jess knew Ava slightly from the local leisure centre, where they both went to swim. They had a sort of passing acquaintance. Sometimes this extended almost to a conversation, but they had always stopped short of getting to know each other better.

A few people on the bridge clapped or cheered when the frogman surfaced and gave his colleagues the thumbs up. Someone next to Jess speculated that this might be 'the murder weapon.' Until that moment, Jess had assumed Leanne had drowned. Her mind reeled at the thought that it might have been murder.

The woman next to her peered into her face. "You alright, duck?"

"I'm fine." Jess managed a small smile.

"Bad business, i'nt it?"

"It is." Jess slipped back into the crowd. She didn't feel fine. Not really. It wasn't that she felt unwell, just slightly detached from reality. It was the way she might feel after drinking in some dimly lit bar at lunchtime and then emerging slightly drunk into the sunshine.

Her mind conjured up an image of two very different teenage girls, one street smart and strong, the other with a disfiguring condition that attracted the derision and cruelty of the school bullies. Leanne and Jess. As an adolescent, Jess had suffered from idiopathic scoliosis, a severe curvature of the spine that twisted her back out of shape, destroying her confidence and isolating her socially at a vulnerable time of her young life.

Leanne had lived on what was, back in the noughties, the most notorious housing estate in Stromford. In many ways she was typical of a kid from such a background. Her conduct in class had been challenging, her attitude to authority figures disrespectful and defiant, and her behaviour with boys precocious. She was like an unstable element, seemingly unable to bind the various atoms of her personality together into a coherent identity. Possibly only Jess knew that Leanne was kind.

Jess had discovered this one lunchtime at school. She had left her pencil case in the art room and gone back to look for it. The art room was located at the end of a long corridor with an alcove for lockers about half way down. Walking past the alcove, Jess had heard a girl call out, "Hey look. It's the spastic. Want to come and play with us, Spaz?"

Jess walked past without turning her head, tears pricking her eyes. She should have been immune to the taunts by then, but it was hard to face them down when you were only thirteen. She retrieved her pencil case and walked past the alcove a second time. The same calls rang out.

Then Leanne was there. "Why don't you pick on someone your own size, Chelsea? Oh, I know why. No one else with an arse big enough." Leanne closed her locker and stared Chelsea Hope down. It was no contest. Chelsea mumbled something about not having anything against Leanne, and she and her two cronies suddenly found they had somewhere else to be.

"Th . . . thanks," Jess stammered, staring down at her shoes.

"No problem. Can't stand bullies. You let me know if they bother you again."

"You . . . your name's Leanne, isn't it?"

"Yeah, that's right. We were in the same class for English last year."

"I remember. You . . . you were good at writing stories."

"Was I? Don't remember that."

"You wrote one about dolphins. It was lovely."

Leanne stared at Jess. "Fancy you remembering that." She seemed on the point of walking away, then hesitated. She asked rather awkwardly, "So what's wrong with you, really? Were you born like that?"

Jess coloured. She was used to people staring but they seldom asked so bluntly.

"I have something called idiopathic scoliosis. No one knows what causes it. It makes my spine grow twisty."

"Does it hurt?"

"Sometimes, but mostly it doesn't."

"Is it curable?"

"I wear a back brace at night to help stop the curve from getting worse. I can have an operation when I'm older to help straighten it out."

"That's good, isn't it?" Leanne said. Jess nodded, uncertainly.

"You shouldn't take any notice of what people say. If anyone calls you names, let me know and I'll take care of them."

And she had. From that day on, Leanne seemed to appear whenever anyone hurled unkind words Jess's way. She heard them all. An endless stream of hurtful, hateful comments that sucked away her confidence and self-esteem throughout her adolescence. Bullying is insidious and enduring. Jess never truly recovered the confidence of her pre-teen years. She recalled her embarrassment in the changing rooms, her efforts to get undressed with her back to the wall so that no one could see her misshapen spine and call her by the worst name of all. Hunchback.

And now Leanne was dead, at twenty-three. Jess felt stricken. Leanne hadn't simply drowned, she had been attacked first. There was a murder weapon. She would have fought back, Jess was sure. Leanne had never been the passive type. She would have fought with every ounce of strength available to her. Imagining what Leanne's final moments must have been like, sinking, bleeding into the dark water, made Jess feel sick to her stomach.

But it wasn't just Leanne's tragic fate that bothered Jess. It was her own shame too. She had not looked out for Leanne the way Leanne had looked out for her. Always difficult, Leanne had gone completely off the rails a couple of years after Jess's encounter with her in the corridor, and had been expelled from school. Jess had only seen her a couple of times after that. The first occasion was in the Riverside shopping centre in Stromford. Leanne was being led out of a clothes store by a security guard, caught shoplifting. Leanne grinned at Jess as she was ushered past, but Jess was with her mother and looked away, embarrassed.

The second time was a couple of years later. Jess, her once misshapen spine newly transformed by surgery, was shopping on the High Street with a friend when a brawl broke out in the street between two young women, arguing over drugs. One of them was a scarcely-recognisable Leanne. A couple of security guards from the nearby shopping centre were struggling to prise the two women apart, when Leanne suddenly looked up and caught Jess's eye. She gave Jess a flicker of a smile but again, Jess had turned away.

Three times Jess betrayed Leanne. The last time was quite recent. A couple of weeks ago she received an email from Leanne on her college email account. Leanne was a student at the college now, and wondered if Jess could spare some time to meet her. Jess had intended to reply, but she'd been busy and somehow she never got around to it.

Jess liked to think of herself as a compassionate person. Her experience of bullying could have made her bitter, but she liked to believe that it had made her more sensitive. But she had turned away from Leanne when she was in trouble. Some caring person she was. Now Leanne was gone and Jess would never have an opportunity to put things right.

Jess crossed the road. She leaned over the other side of the bridge and saw more police activity — officers searching the paths on either side of the river, and the marina.

"Oh, Leanne. How did you end up in that river?" Jess asked aloud.

"What's that, duck? Who was you talking to?" It was a homeless man with a curious little dog at his side wearing a dirty check scarf.

Jess turned towards them. "Just thinking aloud."

"You wasn't thinking of jumping in, was you?" the beggar asked. His dog gave a yap and licked its master's hand.

"Definitely not."

"Good then. They pulled a poor young lass out of there last night. Police asked me if I'd seen anything."

"Oh." Jess's heart quickened. "Did you?"

"Not a thing. Hardly surprising, seeing as I was tucked up in the Centre that time of night. Bright Night Centre down Rampton Lane. Know it?" Jess nodded. "Nice place," the man said, stroking his dog. "They don't mind me bringing Victor here in. Long as he don't sleep on the bed."

Jess waited for him to say something else, but he seemed to have lost interest in the conversation and was rolling a cigarette. The dog limped over to Jess and she bent to pet him. Poor thing, he only had three legs. She stood for a moment longer, gazing at the river, feeling the bridge vibrate with the passing vehicles. Below, the river was teeming with colourless fish — perch and carp and speckled trout — all writhing in the brownish water. Jess walked away.

She had been surprised to see Ava Merry at the scene, though Jess knew she was some sort of police officer. A detective, it appeared, for she wasn't in uniform. Maybe she could speak with her at the pool. Even in swimming hat and goggles Ava managed to look good.

Jess sighed, thinking of the long scar on her back that even her high-backed swimsuit couldn't hide. All through her teenage years she had been so self-conscious about her twisted spine that she had assumed she was ugly. The hunchback. She'd never gone out with boys. Even the seemingly nice ones who told her they didn't care about her back weren't to be trusted. She'd once been persuaded to go out with a boy in the year above her, only to discover that he'd asked her out as a dare. After that it seemed easier not to bother.

Just recently she had started seeing a man called Mitch. Jess couldn't quite believe that he really wanted to be with her. She had shown Mitch a picture of her twisted spine the night they made love for the first time, a medical photograph taken before her operation. He gasped. She sat up, ready to move away, but Mitch pulled her towards him, saying she'd misunderstood him. He ran his fingers the length of her scar, brought his lips to her spine and kissed it.

"Jess!" Jess spun around and came face to face with a man she thought she recognised from somewhere.

"Jonty Cole. I'm Barney's big brother." He held out his hand. He was the brother of one of the students she supported at work. She'd seen him at the college with Barney but she didn't think they'd ever spoken.

"I saw you on the bridge just now," Jonty said. "Terrible, isn't it? You look shaken. Did you know her?"

Was it so obvious? "I . . . Yes, I did."

"I'm so sorry. Were you close?"

"No. We were at school together, but I hadn't seen her for a while."

"Would you like to talk about it? I mean, I know I don't know you very well, but, well, you're Barney's teacher and he absolutely adores you. Anyone Barney likes, I like too."

Jess smiled and shook her head. "I'm fine, honestly. I have a day off work today and I'm going to go home and have a coffee with my neighbour, Pam. She's a kind of second mum to me."

"That's nice," Jonty said. "I'm glad you've got someone. I hate to think of you going home alone and upset."

She thought he'd go then, but he lingered, falling into step beside her until they reached the junction.

"I'm going this way," Jess told him, stopping at the traffic lights. She pointed along the street. "I live just down here. It was nice talking to you, Jonty."

"Likewise. I'll look out for you at the college?" Jess heard the question and wasn't sure how to answer, but just then the lights changed, and she smiled at him and crossed the road. She didn't look back but she had an uneasy feeling that if she did, she would see him still standing there, watching her.

Chapter Three

Jonty Cole stood for a while watching Jess cross the road. He considered following her to find out exactly where she lived, but he was afraid she'd turn around. *How much did she really know?* he wondered. When he'd spotted her on the bridge, his first thought was that Leanne must have contacted her. Why else would she be there? Curiosity? It was possible. Plenty of other people had gathered to gawp.

He churned over the facts in his mind. Jess hadn't seemed afraid of him. She'd acted like she didn't even recognise him, the bitch, yet he'd actually spoken with her more than once about Barney. Either she was a very cool customer and doing a fucking brilliant job of lying through her teeth or she really didn't have a monkey's. Which was it? One thing was certain, if Jess Stokes hadn't been Barney's favourite support worker, she'd already be dead.

Not for the first time, Jonty wondered if he'd acted in haste. Leanne wasn't even onto him. It was Seth she'd been after. How the hell had things got so messy? He knew why, of course. It had been a bad move to get involved with Seth Conway again. At first, their partnership had seemed like the perfect solution to his problems. Then that bitch Leanne had gone on her bloody crusade to right the wrongs of the past and bring Seth Conway to justice. Jonty gave a bitter laugh. He'd gone out with Leanne for a while when they were just kids. He learned then that she wasn't a victim. It hadn't taken her long to get shot of him when she realised what he was. If only he'd had the guts to take care of her back then, he could have saved himself all this mess.

Just the thought of Seth made him feel like heaving. Where did he think he got off threatening him, Jonty? His words rang in Jonty's ear, drowning out the noise of the traffic.

"If I go down, I take you with me."

Jonty knew then that he should cut his losses. He could have dealt with Seth easily enough, but their arrangement was so convenient. He was reluctant to let it go.

There was nothing to prove that Leanne had been in touch with Jess. Jess had not been one of the girls in Seth's group all those years ago. She couldn't be a witness, or testify. But she was in Leanne's mobile phone contact list. No messages, just her name. Had Leanne deleted the thread of their conversation?

Jonty came to a decision. For now he would allow Jess Stokes to live. For Barney's sake. Only for Barney, he told himself. But there was another reason, one that he chose not to dwell on. Jess Stokes interested him. Immensely.

His feelings for Jess had taken him by surprise. Not since he'd fancied Annabelle Rivers at school had he felt anything at all for another person — except for Barney. He recalled how Annabelle had laughed at him when he asked her out. It had never entered his head that a timid mouse like Annabelle would actually reject him. He was Jonty Cole, the sensitive lad who looked out for his poor disabled brother. Most girls loved that he was so good with Barney. Well, he'd miscalculated with Annabelle. He'd had his revenge, though. Even now the knowledge that he was the cause of Annabelle Rivers' limp made him smile.

And the beauty of it was that no one had ever suspected him of hurting her. Not even Annabelle herself. When a girl was involved in an accident, no one ever suspected the nice blokes like Jonty.

His feelings for Jess confounded him because he'd never expected to feel that way about a woman again. It wasn't about sex. He never had a problem with that. Besides, there were the girls Seth gave him access to. Who cared if some of them weren't quite right in the head? There was nothing wrong with their bodies.

It was Barney who'd made him notice Jess. His brother had a crush on her. This was a problem. He'd miss his support worker if things didn't go according to plan. Ah well, Jonty would deal with Barney when the time came, just like he always did.

Barney was Jonty's Achilles heel, and he didn't need another. If Jess turned out to be a second Annabelle, he'd get rid of her. Jonty didn't take rejection lightly.

He didn't resent his 'special' little brother. Barney wasn't hard work, not really. He liked the way Barney loved him unconditionally, the way he hugged him and meant it.

No, what Jonty had resented was the fact that the care had been expected of him. Almost from the day Barney was born, Jonty became his caregiver. His parents had explained to him that Barney was 'special' and that he would always need looking after. One day, when they were too old to look after Barney themselves, Jonty would have to take their place.

He was five when Barney was born. It was the day Jonty's childhood ended.

By the time he started secondary school, Jonty was beginning to lose friends because he was always rushing home to see to his brother. Sometimes the other kids made fun of him over it.

Time and time again, he heard them say, 'Jonty's babysitting his retard brother again.' It made him seethe with anger.

One Saturday morning he was walking along the High Street with Barney when he overheard a particularly cruel remark. It came from two girls from his class — Kelsey White and Courtney Lane. Even now, he could still see their stupid, sneering faces.

"I just lost it." It was the only justification Jonty could summon for what he did to those girls, Kelsey especially, before some passers-by pulled him off.

Kelsey needed stitches to her face. She lost a couple of teeth and had had extensive bruising. There was a lot of blood, and a lot of screaming. Amidst all the commotion, Jonty had been aware of Barney's anguished cries of distress. It had taken two men to restrain the ten-year-old boy.

His mother called it 'kicking off,' as in, "Watch out, Barney's kicking off again." Jonty knew how to calm his brother down, but on that occasion he too was being restrained. Worse still, he had been the cause of Barney's distress. He should have walked away from those girls like he usually did. Instead, he had to stand by and watch helplessly as a couple of burly men wrestled his brother to the ground.

"Fucking psycho!" A paramedic was helping Courtney stand and walk slowly away. She spat at him. "Fucking freak. Just like your brother."

A policeman had appeared, and bystanders were giving statements.

"He just went for them out of the blue."

"Never seen anything like it. Just set on them like a wild animal."

"Two young girls."

"Look what he did to her face."

"Crazy bastard."

And on and on. Jonty heard it all through a thin mist. Barney lay on the ground, in the throes of a fit, with another paramedic tending to him. Jonty understood Barney better now, the way his little brother felt when he 'kicked off.' Barney's rage was all about frustration, his inability to make sense of the world around him and articulate his feelings. But Jonty hadn't expected the exhilaration his own rage brought.

In the days and weeks after the incident, Jonty found himself replaying it over and over in his head. It took some time for his pleasure to diminish. He told himself there was only one way to achieve that level of intensity again. He would have to hurt other women.

Jonty knew he couldn't simply go out and beat up women in the street. He did try it a couple of times, on some homeless druggies. He made do with a succession of weak girlfriends, lowlifes as he liked to think of them, girls no one cared about, who wouldn't complain about being knocked about a bit because even that was preferable to no attention at all.

But it wasn't enough. Jonty wanted to beat his girls to a bloody pulp. But how to go about it? How to take the next step and not be caught?

Then he met Seth.

Jonty attended a party organised by Seth and his friend Henry, who was introduced to Jonty as the 'captain.' It was held on one of those long canal boats.

Over the sound of loud, pulsing music, Seth had shouted, "This is Jasmine. She'll do whatever you want." Jasmine was scantily dressed, dark-eyed and pear-shaped. She gave him a slow, seductive smile, but in her eyes Jonty saw something trapped and fearful. It made him want to hurt her. He led the girl into a tiny cabin and closed the door.

Less than half an hour later, Seth burst in and pulled him off her, alerted by the girl's screams. Jonty's shirt was dishevelled and bloody.

Seth's exclamations of horror brought the captain to the cabin door. When he turned back to Jonty, his face was livid.

"Get off my boat."

Jonty hesitated, and looked to Seth for support.

"Now!" Seth took Jonty by the arm and jostled him up the stairs to the deck.

"What the hell were you thinking?" he asked. Jonty stared at him, genuinely puzzled.

"You said—"

"I didn't say to beat her half to death. A bit of rough stuff, that's all I meant."

Define 'rough stuff,' Jonty wanted to yell.

"What the hell are you anyway, a fucking psycho?"

It was all Jonty could do to keep from jumping on Seth and battering him. Instead, he jumped onto the towpath and strode away towards Stromford.

For a few days he was afraid of repercussions. He'd gone too far with that girl, much further than he'd intended. The sight of her blood spraying over his shirt as he burst her nose had sent him into a frenzy. He hadn't wanted to stop. He'd had to punch the wall a couple of times to stop himself killing her. If Seth hadn't intervened . . .

For a couple of days afterwards he expected to hear from Seth, but he never did. There followed a few years of restraint and intense frustration. Jonty tried — for Barney's sake. What would happen to Barney if he went too far and got himself put away? He'd gone back to giving selected girls a beating, always careful, always holding back.

Then he met Seth again.

Barney loved musicals, and he loved Lex Thorner, a local lad made good. Thorner made a guest appearance at a night club in town, and Jonty introduced them. While Barney listened to Lex singing that famous song from *Les Mis*, Jonty gazed around the room and his eyes alighted on Seth Conway.

Seth didn't recognise Jonty at first. It had been a few years, and he'd been a boy the last time they met. Now he was a man. Jonty reminded him about where they'd last met. They got talking and Jonty saw an opportunity.

When you know all about someone's secret life, it's almost too easy to blackmail them.

"Alright, so what do you want to keep your mouth shut?" Jonty knew that people like Seth never changed, so to add weight to his threat, he hinted that he knew things about Seth's current activities.

Jonty smiled. "You couldn't afford it. But there is a service you can provide for me. I think we could come to an agreement that might benefit us both."

And so, they entered into an uneasy alliance. Every so often, Seth invited Jonty to a party and left him alone with a girl. He even took care of her when Jonty was finished — in his other life he was a nurse. Typically she would have some kind of mental problem, so no one would notice — or care — if she was injured. People with mental health problems are the new lepers, Jonty said to himself, thinking of his brother and how people looked away. They were shunned, invisible. People were either afraid of them or simply didn't want to know about their problems.

Then that bitch Leanne spoiled everything with her snooping. Jonty told Seth not to panic, that he'd take care of it, but Seth baulked. So Jonty had to do it alone.

Chapter Four

Tom Knight refused to park their unmarked car anywhere near where Leanne Jackson's mother lived. It was a new BMW, but at the end of the day it was police issue.

"What?" he said, catching PJ's amused look. "You wouldn't leave your baby somewhere it might get hurt, would you?"

"I don't have a baby."

"Yeah, well, this little beauty is like a baby to me, and I'm not leaving her on this estate to get scratched up by some smartass kid with a shank. I know what I'm talking about from personal experience." He caught PJ's eye again. "Yeah, that's right. Before you ask, I mean personal experience as in I did it myself back in the day."

PJ grinned. "We all have skeletons in our closets."

"Doubt it in your case."

"Huh. Think I'm Little Miss Prim and Proper, do you?"

"Er . . . yes?"

PJ raised her chin. "I've done stuff."

It was Tom's turn to be amused. "What sort of stuff?"

"Just . . . stuff."

"Yeah, right."

Sometimes it irritated PJ that people judged her by her looks. She had brown wavy hair and a round cherubic face, and the kind of body that once would have been called voluptuous. She was also sweet-natured, which reinforced the angelic image. PJ often wished she could be more like Ava. Her friend and colleague was blonde and feminine but she still managed to kick ass. No one would ever accuse Ava of being 'sweet.'

Still, PJ knew that there was a vulnerable side to Ava. No doubt it was this combination of toughness and vulnerability that made her so appealing to men.

"This is it." She stopped at a broken fence, beyond which lay a neglected garden, strewn with rubbish. A grey wheelie bin lay on its side partially blocking the path to the front door. PJ stepped around it, wincing at the sight of maggots wriggling among the pickings of a takeaway pizza.

"Shit. I hate bloody maggots." Tom's face mirrored PJ's.

"At least we agree about something. Oh God, the smell's gonna make me puke." She took a large white handkerchief out of her pocket and put it to her nose, withdrawing it quickly when an angry face poked through the half-opened door.

"Who the fook are you?" His eyes darted from PJ to Tom and back.

"Police, mate." Tom discreetly flashed his ID card. "We're looking for Tina Jackson."

"What the fook do you lot want with our Tina?"

Tom ignored the question. "Is Mrs Jackson inside?"

The man turned away but left the door open. Tom looked at PJ and shrugged. "Ladies first."

"If you were truly chivalrous, you'd insist on going first to protect me. If there's maggots outside the house, who knows what horrors might be lurking inside."

"Exactly," Tom retorted.

The hallway carpet was shiny and smelled of ammonia. "Dog?" PJ whispered.

"Hope so. Alternative's grim."

Their host had disappeared, but a door at the end of the hall stood open. It led into a dimly lit living room. The man had placed himself behind a two-seater sofa, and was leaning with his arms outstretched over the back. On the sofa sat a stick-thin woman with the ravaged face of an alcoholic. Limp, shoulder-length hair, brittle as dried seaweed, framed a face blooming with broken capillaries. She gave PJ and Tom a bleary-eyed look over the rim of her lager can.

Tom cleared his throat. "Mrs Jackson?"

The woman belched and nodded, lowering the can shakily to the arm of the sofa. "I told the copper who came earlier everything I know."

"I'm sorry for your loss, Mrs Jackson."

"I ain't. Little cunt meant nothing to me. Good riddance, I say."

Her words took PJ by surprise. "We're talking about your daughter—" She checked herself. They needed Tina Jackson to cooperate.

"May we?" Tom nodded at another two-seater sofa facing Tina. Tina gave a disinterested nod and Tom and PJ sat down, sinking almost to the floor on the sagging cushions.

"We're aware that you and Leanne were estranged," Tom began.

Tina glared at him. "What's that mean, estranged? Talk English."

"You and your daughter didn't talk."

"Ain't seen 'er for years. We wasn't good enough for 'er. Became quite the lady after she'd done 'er time, or so I 'eard. Never come near me, ungrateful cow."

Leanne Jackson had served time for brawling in the street, resisting arrest and being in possession of an illegal substance. Since then, she'd somehow managed to turn her life around. It was quite a feat considering she hadn't exactly started from a level playing field. *If she really hasn't seen her daughter for years, it's unlikely she'll be of much help,* PJ thought.

Tom coughed again. "Okay, so you haven't been in contact with your daughter recently. Is there any other information you could give us that might help us with our investigation?"

Tina put her head back and drank, raised her backside off the sofa and broke wind loudly. "Needed that." It was unclear whether she meant the alcohol or the fart. "What did you say? Oh, yeah, Leanne. Search me. Right little madam, she was, from the start. Couldn't do a thing wiv her. All the other kids around here was happy to sit in front of the telly all day, but not our Leanne. Then when she hit eleven or twelve, she was proper out of control."

"Did she upset a lot of people, do you know? Make enemies?" PJ asked.

Tina rolled her eyes. "You kidding me? She pissed off everyone she met."

"What about boyfriends?"

"She was a little whore, so yeah, plenty of boyfriends, if that's what you'd call them."

"Right." PJ took a breath.

"I wouldn't know who she's seen recently, would I? There was one as used to knock her about a bit. He was in her anger management group when she were about fourteen." She snorted. "Anger managed her right well."

Like Tina could care less, PJ thought. "Can you remember the boy's name, Mrs Jackson?"

"No idea, duck. Why? D'you reckon it was 'im as done her in?"

"No, we're just trying to . . . I mean, we're just considering possibilities." PJ doubted whether it was worth pursuing, but she jotted it down in her notebook anyway.

"Mr Jackson? Do you have anything to add? You've been very quiet."

Tina snorted. "'E ain't me 'usband. No point asking 'im owt about Leanne. 'E never set eyes on 'er, duck."

"Name's Brian Carlyle," the man said.

"Brian Carlyle." PJ wrote down his name, thinking it would be a miracle if his fingerprints didn't appear somewhere in a police database.

"Just one more thing, was Leanne in contact with her father? And do you know his present whereabouts?" Tom asked.

"That's two things." They waited patiently while Tina recovered from her joke. "An' yeah, I do know of his whereabouts." She paused and smirked at Brian. PJ guessed what was coming. "'E's out back. Buried 'im in the garden 'bout six years ago. Riddled with cancer, bless 'im."

"Right, well, thanks for your time, folks." Tom turned to PJ. "Any more questions, Detective Jenkins?"

PJ shook her head. She thought of asking Tina if she had ever loved her daughter, but the answer was depressingly obvious.

They saw themselves out, sidestepping the prone wheelie bin and its trail of slimy inhabitants.

Tom let out a low whistle of relief when they saw that the car was still where they had left it. PJ strapped herself in while Tom did a quick check for scratches. Thank goodness her Steve wasn't so precious about his car.

Their next destination was Leanne Jackson's last known address. They had obtained her address from the electoral register. When PJ and Tom arrived, forensics were going through the property. The landlord was hovering around but he soon made himself scarce.

PJ had once rented a terraced house similar to this with a friend, and the layout was familiar. The door opened into a narrow hall with stairs on one side and a door leading into a small living room overlooking the street. The room was minimalist rather than homely, furnished throughout with items from IKEA. Tom ran his fingers over the books on a shelving unit. PJ guessed he was someone for whom books held no more than a passing interest.

"All arranged alphabetically by subject, by the looks of them."

"What did she do for a living?" PJ asked.

"She worked for a trust that provides training and employment for people with mental health issues and learning disabilities or recovering from illness, addiction, that sort of thing. The Yeardsley Trust. It's on a small industrial estate off Stonebridge Road."

PJ nodded. "I know it. Actually, my neighbour's brother used to go there. He's got bipolar disorder. He did carpentry and made stuff that the Trust sold." PJ gazed at a rectangular outline in the dust on a small beech desk. "Forensics have already taken her laptop, I see."

They moved to the kitchen. The work surfaces were completely clear of clutter. Leanne had not been absent for long, and there was some food in the fridge that was still fresh. Tom opened a couple of cupboards. Everything was lined up and grouped by type.

"She liked her tuna fish." PJ eyed the neatly stacked cans. Upstairs they found two small bedrooms. One, barely roomy enough to accommodate a single bed, was being used mainly for storage. An ironing board stood in one corner with a basket of clean laundry on the floor by its side. All neatly folded up, waiting to be ironed. Items of underwear and tights and a couple of pairs of jeans were hanging, completely dry, over a clothes horse. A white Billy bookcase was neatly stacked with storage boxes and files.

PJ peered into one of the boxes. It was full of different coloured A4-sized plastic wallets, all with printed labels indicating what was inside — insurance policies, energy bills, certificates, instruction manuals. PJ thought of the chaotic state of her own affairs at home and reminded herself to get organised.

Tom picked up a loose folder and held out a single sheet of paper. "Look at this. Only thing that's not tidied away."

PJ joined him and peered over his shoulder. It was a list of names in alphabetical order. All of them were highlighted in yellow and encircled by a huge question mark. At the top of the page was the word, 'Victims?'

PJ frowned. "Chantelle Clarke. I remember reading about her in the Courier last month. My auntie Susan showed me the article. She was a friend of Chantelle's mother. Terribly sad case. She committed suicide. Had a history of depression and self-harming and had attempted to kill herself several times."

"What method did she use?" Tom asked.

"Pills. Anti-depressants."

"Do you recognise any of the other names?" Tom asked.

PJ read them out. "Alyssa Ballard, Michaela Howard, Ruby Kennedy, Corinna Masters." She shook her head. "What is this list anyway? Is it something Leanne's brought home from work, do you think? Chantelle could well have attended a place like the Yeardsley Trust. We should probably check out the other highlighted names, just in case."

"Absolutely." Tom rolled his neck as if releasing tension. He looked around. "Leanne had a touch of OCD, d'ye reckon?"

"Maybe. Maybe that's why she chose to work at a place like the Yeardsley. She'd feel she fitted in."

Tom pocketed the list. "Let's go. There's nothing here that's shouting at me."

* * *

Ava asked the bartender to open a tab so that she could buy drinks for her colleagues as they trickled in. After the day's dark proceedings, a few drinks would go a long way to lightening the general mood. PJ smiled at Ava over the top of her glass, and beckoned her over to the table where she was sitting with Tom Knight and Dan from forensics. Jim Neal was expected to make an appearance at some point in the evening, though Ava suspected it would be brief. His son, Archie, tended to take priority over social gatherings, and she knew that his friend, Jock, was visiting from Scotland.

Ava sipped her cocktail through a thin, pink straw.

PJ fumbled in her handbag, accidentally elbowing Ava's arm so that her drink slopped.

"Oops, sorry, Ava. Bit too eager." PJ had a reputation for being klutzy, which was sometimes endearing, sometimes exasperating. She passed Ava her notebook, open at a list of names.

"Tom and I visited Leanne Jackson's place earlier. She had a place for everything and then some. This was the only thing we found lying around."

Ava skimmed through the list of names.

"We wondered if Leanne got herself killed over something she was trying to find out."

PJ, newly appointed to her role as detective constable, was eager to show that she deserved the title. Was she jumping to fanciful conclusions? Ava's eyes sought Tom's but he was non-committal.

"Hmm . . . Got anything more to support your theory, Peej?"

"Don't you recognise any of the names on the list?"

Ava ran her eyes over the list again. "Er . . . nope."

"Chantelle Clarke?" PJ prompted. Ava gave her friend a blank look. Sometimes PJ forgot that not everyone had lived in Stromford as long as she had. She would pick up on items of news because she knew someone who knew someone who had been affected by the issues. PJ explained about Chantelle's suicide, but it was the suggestion that she might have attended the Yeardsley Trust that piqued Ava's interest.

"Forensics have got Leanne's laptop," said Tom. "I'll check in with them tomorrow to see if there's any more info on the names on the list."

A couple of drinks later the mood became lighter. Ava found herself knocking back drink after drink as her colleagues repaid her generosity behind the bar. At one point there were four cocktails lined up in front of her. It wasn't long before she began to live up to her surname.

Ava declared she was "thoroughly pissed."

"Serves you right for being so popular," PJ observed.

Ava performed a couple of Lady Gaga songs on the karaoke. Amidst cries of 'encore' and cheering, she got up to perform a third. She'd kicked off her shoes, stripped down to her red strappy top, let her blonde hair tumble from its ponytail and was drunkenly twerking away when a movement at the door caught her eye. Ava turned in time to see DI Neal's stern face rearrange itself into an awkward smile that threatened to become a laugh.

"And my next number is for Jim Neal!" Ava yelled, drunkenly. "Let's hear it for the boss!"

Before she could launch into her next song, someone wrestled the microphone from her grasp.

"Let's hear it for Detective Sergeant Ava Merry." PJ's voice filtered through a sort of fug. At the sound of hearty hand-clapping and cheering, she took a bow and, leaning heavily on PJ, made it back to their table. "Glad you could make it, Jimmy Boy!" She gave Neal a hearty slap on the back. PJ rolled her eyes, Dan grinned and Tom Knight smirked.

Ava reached for her glass but PJ swiped it deftly away. "Come on, Ava. You've had enough for now." Ava was about to protest when the whole room started to spin and she felt everything fall away backwards.

She clutched PJ. "Oh no! I think I'm going to puke."

Tom Knight was on his feet in a flash, not in gallantry, but to avoid the vomit he evidently feared was on its way.

PJ grabbed Ava by the arm. "Oh no, you're not. You just hold that a minute till we get to the Ladies." She steered Ava expertly across the floor. Moments later she was obligingly holding those blonde tresses out of the way while Ava threw up.

"Bloody hell, Ava. At least try to get it in the pan."

"S . . . sorry. Oh God, Peej. Have I made a complete arse of myself in front of everyone?"

"Only in the last five minutes or so, if you don't count your Lady Gaga impersonation. Oh, and belting DI Neal on the back." She handed Ava a wad of toilet paper. "Here. You've got sick on your chin."

When they made it back to their seats, the three men nodded politely. PJ picked up Ava's jacket and draped it around her friend's shoulders. "I'm going to call Ava a cab."

Neal began to stand up. "No need. I'll drive her home."

"Are you sure, sir?" PJ asked.

"No problem, PJ. Is that alright with you, Merry?"

"Yessir. Thank you, sir." Ava just hoped she wouldn't throw up in his car.

Outside, the fresh air made her feel slightly better. "I don't normally drink a lot. Must have lost count. People kept buying me cocktails. I couldn't very well not drink them, could I?"

Neal smiled. "It would have been impolite, I suppose. Here we are." He helped her into the passenger seat and leaned over her to fasten her seatbelt, brushing against her breasts as he did so. Ava gave a little moan and smiled at him.

"You're a very sexy man, Jim Neal." She leaned back against the headrest, thinking it would be nice if he were to kiss her, but it would also be nice if she could focus on his face properly.

"And you're very drunk," Neal replied. He started up the car. Ava was asleep in seconds.

* * *

Neal was glad to see a light still on when they arrived at her cottage. He left Ava sleeping in his car while he went to the door and knocked.

He and her brother Ollie helped Ava inside the cottage and onto a sofa. Neal suspected she would sleep there until morning.

Back in his car, straightening the seatbelt on the passenger side, he thought of the moment when he had brushed against Ava, and how she had given that little moan of pleasure and it made his pulse quicken. It would have been so easy to lean over and kiss her. He was sure she wouldn't have remembered it in the morning.

Neal arrived home around midnight and, as he expected, his friend, Jock Dodds, was still up, drinking whisky and evidently in maudlin mood.

"I'm in love with Maggie."

Neal sighed. It was hardly a shocking revelation. Jock Dodds had held a torch for Neal's sister Maggie since he was a boy of sixteen. A few months before, Maggie, who lived with Neal and his son Archie, had nearly died at the hands of a crazed killer. Neal had been wondering if this incident would give Jock a kick up the pants and make him act on his feelings. And about time too.

"Aye. The question is, what are you going to do about it?"

Jock held up his glass. "Half full, or half empty?"

"Just talk to her, man." Neal could understand Jock's dilemma. Lose a friend or gain a lover? Neal reckoned the odds were in Jock's favour.

Jock sighed. He lifted his glass with his left hand and conveyed it awkwardly to his mouth. The arm was encased in plaster. He had been involved in an accident a couple of weeks before and had required surgery on his arm and shoulder. There was the possibility of nerve damage. "I'm thinking of changing my specialism."

Neal nodded. "Psychiatry?"

"Aye. It's not just this." Jock looked down at his arm. He had spoken before about his interest in psychiatry. Neal suspected the injury was not the sole deciding factor. No wonder his friend was drunk. He was up against two major life decisions.

"It would mean a bit of retraining, of course."

Neal sensed Jock wanted to talk. He was happy to listen. After the sudden death of his parents in a car accident, Jock's family had taken him in. He and Jock had become more like brothers than friends. Maggie had gone to live with an aunt, but they had all been close growing up.

These days it was rare for them to spend time together. The demands of their careers meant that neither had the time to travel between Stromford and Edinburgh. There was the odd walking trip whenever they could fit it in, but Neal also had parental responsibilities and free time was a luxury.

This time Jock had no need to rush back to Edinburgh. He was on sick leave, awaiting further surgery on his arm. "Stay a bit longer," Neal urged. "Maggie will be delighted."

Jock smiled and held up his glass. "Half full."

Chapter Five

Home for Jess was a small flat in a Victorian conversion on a long sloping street lined with cherry trees and parked cars. She had been surprised to discover that the rent was just within her budget. She'd been lucky with her neighbours too. The house had been split into three flats. Magda, a Polish woman, lived on the ground floor, opposite Jess. She worked as a care assistant at a care home. The first floor flat was occupied by a woman in her fifties, Pam Hollis, who had recently left her husband and was renting until her divorce was settled. Pam's current soul mate was a three-year-old chocolate Labrador called Bunty. Jess loved Bunty almost as much as Pam did and enjoyed their long walks across the west common on Saturday mornings. If Magda wasn't working, she'd come too, and more often than not the three of them would end up in a little coffee shop on the edge of the common.

Feeling troubled after hearing of Leanne's death, Jess felt a sudden need for company and decided to call on Pam. She climbed the stairs to Pam's part of the house. Pam was delighted to see her.

"I hope I'm not keeping you from working," Jess said.

"Absolutely not. I need a break before I get started." Now in her mid-fifties, Pam had reinvented herself as a writer, self-publishing romantic fiction that Jess often had the privilege of reading first. Jess stepped inside and made a fuss of an excited Bunty, while Pam put the kettle on.

Pam's flat was bigger than Jess's and reflected a lifetime of gathering objects around her. She had a lot of books and had invited Jess to borrow whatever took her fancy. Jess followed Bunty into Pam's living room and was drawn immediately to the big bay window looking out over the west common. Pam's writing desk was positioned to take full advantage of the vista from the window. With a view like this, Jess marvelled that Pam ever got any work done. The west common was a vast swathe of grassland extending outwards from the city into the surrounding countryside. Ponies roamed freely across its wide expanse, which was dotted with shrubberies and recreational facilities, and of course dogs and their owners. Miraculously, it still managed to look wild and unmanaged.

"Admiring the view?" Pam smiled. "Bunty's been gazing longingly at it for the past half hour. I think I'll have to quit working and take her for a walk after our coffee."

When Jess turned from the window, she was blinking back tears.

"Are you alright, sweetie?"

"Two students found a young woman in the river last night," Jess answered.

"Yes, I heard about it on the news earlier." Pam looked at Jess.

"I knew her. Her name was Leanne Jackson. I was at school with her. She was kind to me when the other kids weren't." Jess had told Pam about the bullying she suffered at school, but she had never mentioned Leanne. So she told Pam about the time in the school corridor when Leanne had intervened on her behalf. "It wasn't just the once, either. She always seemed to be nearby when the other kids were taunting me."

"She sounds like a kind person. You say she wasn't exactly a model student? She was disruptive? Her behaviour was probably masking some trouble of her own."

"I think she had a pretty difficult home life. There were rumours that her mum was an alcoholic or a junkie."

Pam looked at her. "There's something else, isn't there?"

Reluctantly, Jess told her about the two occasions she had ignored Leanne when she was in trouble.

"There was nothing you could have done," Pam reassured her. "I understand why you feel guilty, but you couldn't have helped her on either of those occasions. Leanne put herself in those situations."

"It's not that, you know it's not. It's the fact that I pretended I didn't even know her. I looked away. She smiled at me and I looked away. Twice. That's not the way a good person behaves."

"It's the behaviour of a normal person. Don't be so hard on yourself, Jess."

"They're saying it was murder. I've been down to the river where her body was found. There were frogmen and they found something that everyone was saying must have been the murder weapon."

"Well, you don't know that for sure. It hasn't been announced that the police are treating it as murder. Obviously it's suspicious, but it's more likely to be some sort of tragic accident. You say it was near the marina? There are a lot of bars along the waterfront area there. Leanne might have had too much to drink and fallen into the river."

Somehow that didn't help. "Well if it was murder, I'm going to find the person who did this to her."

Pam looked worried. "No you're not. You're not a vigilante, Jess. Let the police do their job."

Jess didn't answer. Her face took on a determined expression. Pam poured some of her tea onto a saucer and put it on the floor for Bunty to lap. She changed the subject.

"How are things going with Mitchell?"

"Okay." Jess was hesitant.

"Just okay?"

Jess told her about her fears that Mitch pitied rather than loved her.

Pam shook her head. "Rubbish. I've seen the way that young man looks at you. Besides, it's early days. You've only been together a few weeks, haven't you?"

Jess nodded. They'd met, quite by chance, in the multi-storey car park one Saturday morning. Mitch had parked his car beside hers and she'd felt a bit uneasy because there had been plenty of other spaces. She'd waited in her car until he went over to the parking meter, then moved to the deck above. But they had encountered each other again on the stairs. He'd been waiting for her.

"What about you, Pam? Don't you ever think about dating again? You're far too young to stay on the shelf."

"I don't want or need a man to look after me, Jess. I'm perfectly happy on my own."

"I didn't mean to suggest that you weren't. It's just that you've got so much to offer. You deserve to love and be loved in return."

"You know the saying. 'Once bitten, twice shy.'"

"Come on. You and Stan had a lovely life together before the cancer. You can't judge all men by Michael."

Pam gave her a withering look.

"Sorry. That sounded a bit patronising, didn't it?"

"A tad." Pam looked thoughtful. "Actually, I might have met someone." She ignored Jess's wide smile. "Just this morning, on the common. It's nothing to get excited about."

"And?"

"He's very nice."

"And?"

"I'll probably see him again."

Jess beamed. "I'm so happy for you, Pam."

"It's early days."

"I know. How did you meet, exactly?"

"I was walking Bunty first thing. He was walking Boris, his borzoi. That's a kind of shaggy greyhound, also known as a Russian wolfhound. He has a beautiful brindled coat. He and Bunty took a real shine to each other."

At last Jess laughed. "I'd love to meet him."

"Well, you will. I'll invite you and Mitchell for dinner, then you can invite Henry and I back. It'll be like Come Dine With Me."

"Thanks, Pam."

"For what, child?"

Pam often called her that. It made Jess feel safe, like being at home again.

"Just thanks, that's all."

Later, back in her own flat, Jess thought about Pam calling her a vigilante. Well, she was no superwoman, but she felt she owed it to Leanne. At the very least she could find out how far the police had got with their investigation. Before going to bed, she set her alarm for six. She wanted to wake up in time to get to the pool and catch DS Merry.

Chapter Six

Ollie shook Ava awake at six. She had a crick in her neck and a thumping headache. She was also fully dressed and lying on the sofa. She frowned.

"What am I doing downstairs?"

"You were drunk. DI Neal brought you home and we thought it would be easier than getting you upstairs."

"Drunk?" Fractured memories of the night before began to appear in her clouded mind. She groaned. "Oh no."

"You look awful. And you smell disgusting." Ollie went back upstairs and a moment later Ava heard the shower running.

At seven thirty she dropped Ollie off at a friend's house and drove to the swimming pool. A couple of paracetamol and a litre of water had reduced the pounding in her head to a steady but manageable ache. Ava completed a vigorous sixty-four lengths, fewer than her usual eighty, but not bad with a hangover. She pulled herself up on to the poolside, feeling reinvigorated.

"Show off!"

Ava looked down to see a red-faced woman grinning up at her. She hadn't noticed Jess while she was tearing up and down, most likely because Jess was across the pool from her in one of the slower lanes.

"Morning, Jess. Good to see you." Jess was another of the pool's morning regulars. She arrived even earlier than Ava and dutifully completed fifty lengths before climbing out and declaring herself to be "knackered." Over the years Ava had exchanged the normal pleasantries with Jess, never finding out her surname or learning very much about her. They both had jobs to rush to.

"Have you got a minute? Not right now, I mean. After your shower? There's something I'd like to ask you about. That's if you have the time?" There was something almost pleading in Jess's tone.

Ava wondered if Jess wished to discuss a police matter. She had once mentioned to Jess that she was a detective. Well, she had time. Besides, she wasn't in any rush to see Jim Neal this morning.

"Sure. Want to meet in the café when you're ready?"

After her shower Ava found Jess sitting at one of the centre's blue-topped tables, overlooking the pool. Jess jumped up as she approached and insisted on buying her a drink. Ava asked for a sobering black coffee and while she waited for Jess to return from the machine, she gazed down at the pool and noticed a group of schoolchildren troop out of the changing rooms and line up at the poolside. One of them was Jim Neal's son, Archie. She raised her hand as though to wave, then lowered it, feeling foolish. There was no way Archie would be able to see her from down there.

Jess handed Ava a paper cup. "You did say no milk, didn't you?"

"Yeah, that's how I like it. Sit down, Jess. You look a bit anxious. Is something wrong?"

Jess seemed to hesitate, and then, sighing deeply, she sat down.

"I saw you down by the river yesterday morning. I was on the bridge, watching the divers." Ava blew on her coffee and waited.

"The thing is, I know . . . knew her, the girl those students found the night before. Leanne Jackson. I heard about her on the morning news and it made me shiver. You don't expect to hear something so shocking about someone you know."

Ava noticed that Jess said she knew Leanne, not that she was a friend. She listened while Jess told her about how Leanne Jackson had helped her when they were schoolgirls. When Jess mentioned her scoliosis, Ava recalled the long scar on Jess's back that she had noticed the very first time she'd seen her. She glanced at Jess's shoulder where the scar began. It was hard to believe that her spine had once been the way she described, bent and twisted out of shape, making her stoop and lean to the side and attract cruel taunts from her schoolmates. Besides the scar, there was no evidence of any of that now. Jess looked strong and healthy. Ava wondered about the other scars, the ones that don't show but often run far deeper. One thing was clear to Ava, Jess carried a heavy burden of guilt for what she saw as her betrayal of Leanne's kindness.

"I'd just like to ask what you know about who killed her. I thought maybe as a detective you'd be able to tell me something other people can't."

Ava shook her head. "I'm not sure I can be of much help."

Jess looked embarrassed. "Oh. I just thought I'd ask, you know. On the off-chance."

"You see, I can't really tell you anything about an ongoing case," Ava said.

Jess gave a small smile. "Oh, I see. I suppose not. I guess there's a confidentiality issue."

"I can reassure you that we'll be doing everything possible to find out what happened to Leanne, if that's of any comfort," Ava added.

Jess stared at her hands. "They found something, didn't they? The diver brought something up from the riverbed. I saw him giving a thumbs up sign. Was it . . . the murder weapon?" Her voice faltered. "Do you think she suffered?"

Yes and yes, Ava thought. She covered Jess's trembling hands with her own. "We don't know how she died yet. I'm so sorry I can't tell you any more at the moment. I'll try to keep you updated."

Jess gazed into her eyes. "I want so much to help. How can I help, Ava?"

"By letting us do our job."

Jess nodded, but Ava knew she wasn't satisfied. "Isn't it strange, Leanne and I, the two of us ending up working in the same sort of field? I wish I'd known. I always thought one day I might . . ." She stared at her untouched drink.

Ava couldn't think of much to say, but she gave Jess a sympathetic smile. She stood up. "I'm sorry but I have to get to work, Jess. I really will try to keep you posted on the investigation as far as I'm able. At least I know where to find you."

Jess's return smile was fleeting. "Can we exchange contact details anyway, just in case I miss a swim?"

Ava took her number and left Jess sitting at the table.

* * *

Jess watched Ava's hurried exit from the café. In her swimsuit she looked lean and athletic. Dressed now in black skinny jeans and a denim jacket, with her hair in a dishevelled bun, she exuded beauty and confidence. Yet Jess also sensed a hidden vulnerability. It was present in her alertness, which could just as easily be read as wariness.

She was already wishing she hadn't spoken to Ava. Should she have bothered someone she hardly knew? Ava Merry was probably a very busy woman. What if she thought Jess was taking advantage of her? After all, they weren't friends. Jess glanced at the clock and grabbed her bag, leaving the coffee unfinished.

Twenty minutes later, she was at work. Barney called out her name and rushed over for a hug. It was how he greeted everyone, including strangers, unfortunately. It was one of Jess's tasks to help him become more aware of social conventions. Barney had no way of assessing any threat or dislike on the part of other people. He trusted everyone. It was a loveable trait and a dangerous one too. Jess looked around for Barney's brother, Jonty, remembering their conversation on the bridge.

"Morning, Jess. Hope you're feeling okay after yesterday." Jonty seemed to appear from nowhere. He ruffled Barney's hair. "It's a pleasure to see Barney's favourite support worker."

Jess laughed. "Everyone's a favourite of Barney's."

"I'm sorry he's late this morning. My fault, isn't it, Barney? He stayed over with me last night and I forgot to set the alarm. He was worried about being late for sports, weren't you, mate?" Barney nodded vigorously.

"What time are we doing sports today, Barney?" Jess was trying, without much success, to help Barney grasp the concept of time.

Barney looked thoughtful, counted his fingers, then said, "Eleven o'clock?"

"And what time is it now?"

Barney consulted his digital watch. "Nine-o-five."

"That's right. Well done, Barney."

Jonty slapped him on the back and Barney beamed.

She smiled. "Plenty of time, Barney. Barney's always telling us about all the great things he does with you. What was it last night? Football? Cinema?"

"Football!" Barney exclaimed. "We won. Free nil."

Jonty looked at his watch. "I've got to get to work now, Barney. Gimme five, big man." The pair high-fived. Jonty gave Jess a broad smile. She could tell he liked her. Jonty seemed nice and he seemed interested in her, but she didn't want to give him any encouragement now that she was with Mitch.

"You'd better watch out. Warden's on the prowl." Jess nodded at Jonty's car, parked just this side of the parking barrier on college property.

The morning passed quickly, as it always did when she was busy. The students' day held plenty of activities. Academic lessons, of course, but also other pursuits designed to equip them with life skills. Jess knew that some of her charges would never achieve true independence. Barney was a case in point. Whatever skills he learned here at college, it was unlikely he would ever be able to look after himself. Nor would he ever be able to work unsupervised. It was her job to help ensure that he reached his potential. Just like any other young man his age.

Jess left the college at two thirty in the afternoon and walked home. She'd been hoping for full-time hours, but her contract was for twenty-eight hours a week. She liked what she did, but realistically she would need to find something else if she were to keep herself afloat financially. As it was, after paying her rent she had little left to live on. The thought of a second job was unappealing. One of these days she would have to consider retraining, upskilling.

Jess walked up the steps to her flat, where her downstairs neighbour, Magda, was struggling to find her keys while juggling an outsized box in her arms. Jess stepped forward, holding out her keys. "I've got it. You concentrate on your parcel."

"Fanks so much, Jess." Magda had a strong Polish accent. Jess held the door.

Magda squeezed past her into the dim hallway. "Oh, my gott!"

As soon as Jess stepped inside, she understood what Magda meant. A putrid stench permeated the downstairs lobby. "What the hell is it?"

"Somefing det, I fink," Magda said.

"Where's it coming from?"

It wasn't a huge hallway. There was really only one place the smell could be coming from. Both women advanced slowly towards the cupboard under the stairs. It held an old bicycle that belonged to Pam and a couple of kitchen chairs stacked one atop the other, some dusty cardboard boxes and a matrix of cobwebs. No one had swept it for a long time.

Jess grimaced. "It's coming from one of the boxes. Shit. We're going to have to take a look. Are any of them yours?"

Magda shook her head. "Chairs are mine. Boxes must be Pam's."

"She must have put them there and forgotten about them. Either that, or something's crawled in there and died."

Magda grasped Jess's arm and pointed to a box crammed into the narrowest point under the stairs. It was wedged in with what looked like a triangular chunk of paving stone. But neither the box nor the stone concerned Jess. It was the stain. Wet and sticky. And still spreading by the looks of the widening dark patch.

Magda tugged at her arm. "Okay. That is blut. We go back."

"No! We have to look."

"I tell you, is nothink good in there. We call police."

Jess took a few tentative steps closer to the box. Then a couple more, wishing she had a stick or an umbrella. The thought of touching whatever was inside made her feel queasy. Magda was right. There must be something dead in there. It wasn't human, obviously. The box was far too small for that. What then? A rat? That was the likeliest explanation. A rat had crawled in there and died. Jess steeled herself and lifted the lid.

The stench made her retch. At her back, Magda gagged and uttered a string of expletives in perfect English.

Jess kicked the now lidless box onto its side and a putrid stew of what looked like some kind of offal slopped out. Heart, liver, intestines, kidneys, brains. It looked as if the innards of several animals had been packaged up, then spilled randomly over the carpet.

Magda squealed. "Fucking sheet!"

"It's just butcher's meat of some sort — offal, I think. Pam probably got it for Bunty and forgot to give it to her, so it's gone rotten. God, but it reeks."

"Like J . . . Jack Reeper," Magda said.

The idea was so ridiculous that Jess burst out laughing. "It's animal bits, not human." But there was no convincing Magda. She had her phone out and was stabbing in the numbers. Nine nine nine.

"Magda! You can't call the police out for something like this. We'll look like idiots. Not only that, you're wasting their time."

"You no understanding," Magda choked. "You not look." She pointed to the foul-smelling mess on the floor and repeated, "Look!"

Jess looked. And saw what she had not seen before. Amidst the offal was something else. She recognised it immediately.

"Oh no!" Jess lurched forwards and stooped to pick up the strip of soft leather, encrusted with three shiny studs. With mounting horror, she turned it over to read the name engraved on the back. 'Bunty.'

Jess took the steps two at a time. Outside Pam's door, she knocked urgently and squinted through the spyhole. Magda joined her, out of breath, just as Pam called out, "Hold your horses. I'm coming."

Hearing a familiar — and totally unexpected — noise on the inside of the door, Jess looked at Magda. She could have swooned with relief. "That's Bunty scratching," she said, beaming.

"Bunty? She is okay?" Magda cried.

Pam appeared, looking puzzled. "Why wouldn't she be?"

"We thought. .." Jess began. What had they thought? It seemed ridiculous now that they had believed someone had slaughtered Bunty and left her innards in a box downstairs.

"What happened to Bunty's dog collar?" Jess asked.

"She's wearing it," Pam said. Jess looked down and saw that Bunty was indeed wearing a collar. A blingy new one with sparkly studs.

"Wait a minute. That's not the one she usually wears, is it?"

"We lost that one when we were out on the common the other day."

"How do you lose a dog collar?" Jess asked.

Pam shrugged. "I let Bunty off the lead for a bit and I was chatting to some other dog walkers. When she came back, her collar was missing. I only took my eyes off her for a minute or so. I assumed the leather had worn through, or she'd scratched it loose or something."

Someone was pounding on the door downstairs. Jess and Magda jumped. "Oh shit. That must be the police," said Jess.

"The police? What on earth's going on with you two?"

Instead of replying, Jess ran downstairs and opened the door. A uniformed officer stood on the doorstep.

"I'm so sorry. I think there's been a misunderstanding—"

"What's that smell?" the policeman interrupted, sniffing. "Bloody hell."

"That's sort of what we called you about," Jess said. "My friend and I thought we'd discovered some body parts in a box under the stairs." She almost giggled. If only Magda hadn't panicked and called the police. The emergency number at that.

"Body parts?" The policeman was already following the smell. "Ah," he said, seeing the upturned box and its reeking contents. He bent down for a closer look. He pointed to the dog collar. "What's this?"

"It's a dog collar." The voice came from the stairwell where Pam had been hovering. Now she came all the way to the bottom of the steps. "It belongs to my dog, I think. What's going on, Jess?"

The officer looked from Pam to the pile of offal and back.

"We thought it was Bunty's . . . organs." Jess said, with an apologetic glance at Pam.

The police officer raised his eyebrows. "Right."

"At first we thought they might be human, that's why my friend called you. We're really sorry for wasting your time, officer." Jess was relieved to see that the police officer did not look annoyed.

Pam chipped in. "Hang on. This could be a serious matter. What's Bunty's collar doing with that lot?"

"I take it none of you know how it got there?" the policeman asked. He peered up the stairwell. Anyone else live here?"

"No. There's just the three flats — mine, Pam's and Magda's."

"How secure is the entry to the flats?"

"We all have a key to the main door. We always keep it locked." Pam and Magda nodded.

"Who else might have access? Husbands? Boyfriends? Partners? Anyone ever lent a key to someone, or given them one to keep?"

All three women shook their heads. Jess was sure Magda sometimes gave her key to her boyfriend but she didn't say anything.

"Anyone have reason to believe that someone might be trying to intimidate them?" He looked at Pam. The dog collar was hers.

"Well, there's my husband, I suppose. We're going through a rather acrimonious divorce, but I'm pretty sure Michael wouldn't pull a stunt like that."

The police officer seemed sceptical. "You'd be amazed at what people are capable of, given the right circumstances. Vengeful partners are the worst." His tone suggested he was speaking from personal experience.

"How can you be sure these are animal organs? I mean, don't you need to take them away and have them examined by one of those forensic people?" Pam asked.

"Looks like something you'd find down the butchers, but it makes sense to treat it as evidence in case there is some funny business going on." The officer took out his radio.

The women retreated upstairs to Pam's flat. Pam took a cup of coffee down to the police officer who was guarding the scene until his colleague came in with an evidence bag.

"This is all a bit creepy," said Pam. Jess and Magda sat together on Pam's comfortable sofa, drinking coffee laced with whisky 'for the shock.'

"Someone has taken collar from your dog, no?" Magda suggested to Pam.

Pam shivered. So did Jess.

"Letting agency has spare keys," Magda pointed out.

"They wouldn't give them out to just anybody." Jess turned to Magda. "If that policeman comes up here, promise you won't mention Jack the Ripper."

The PC brought back his empty coffee cup. "My partner's had a quick look and he's pretty sure they're an animal's organs. Most likely it's the sort of mixed bag you can buy over the counter at the butcher's, but we will check that out." He looked at all of them in turn. "That doesn't mean we won't take the matter seriously. If it's a hoax of some sort, it's in very poor taste. It might be a good idea for you to be more mindful of security. Do you have a personal alarm?" He looked to Pam.

"I don't need one. I have a dog." Bunty wagged her tail.

The PC looked at Bunty. "Is she always with you?"

"Point taken."

"You should all have one." Magda pulled a rape alarm from her handbag and the PC gave her an approving smile. "Right, well. Keep us advised of any further incidents."

After he'd gone, Jess nagged Pam about buying an alarm. "It wouldn't hurt any of us to be a bit more security conscious. I'm going to ring the letting agency and see if they can persuade the landlord to get the locks changed."

Magda looked sceptical. "Huh. Good luck with dat. Still I am waiting for repair to bathroom tap."

"What about your ex, Pam? You said he wouldn't do such a thing, but can you really be sure? And what about this Henry you're seeing? How well do you know him?" Jess looked at Pam.

"Michael wouldn't do a thing like that. It's not his style. And I'm not exactly 'seeing' Henry. We've only just met. It's just a prank. Someone's idea of a laugh. It could be anyone, really. Lots of people know I've got a dog called Bunty. Maybe one of them found the collar and decided to play a sick joke."

Jess sighed. "You're probably right. Any chance of a top up?"

Pam picked up the bottle of scotch. "No point diluting it. I'll get some glasses."

By the time Jess got back to her flat, she was feeling slightly drunk. As she fumbled with her key in the lock, she felt a prickling sensation, as though she were being watched. She turned round and Mitch stepped out of the door alcove. "Mitch! You scared the shit out of me! How did you get in? Wasn't the outside door locked?"

"Sorry for scaring you, babe. The door was ajar. Someone must have forgotten to lock it." He sniffed the air. "Smelly in here today."

Jess invited him in. "We've had a bit of an episode. The police were here. We must all have forgotten about locking the door in the excitement."

Mitch looked at her. "What kind of an episode?"

Jess told him about the smell, the bag of organs. He looked troubled. "So . . . Do you think it was Pam's ex — what's his name, Michael?"

"I don't know. It seems the most likely explanation." Mitch gazed at her with a worried expression. "What? What're you thinking, Mitch?"

"People who do this sort of thing . . ." Mitch's voice trailed off.

"What? Tell me what you were going to say."

"Well, sometimes this sort of thing can escalate, you know, like with people who start fires." Mitch was a fireman. He was always telling her stories about arsonists and how their behaviour often followed a particular pattern. According to him, a lot of serial killers began life as arsonists or animal torturers. He rubbed his chin. "I don't like this, Jess. It's sinister. Maybe I should move in for a bit, keep a closer eye on you."

Jess shook her head. "I think you're overreacting. No one's been hurt, and the more I think about it, the more I'm convinced it was probably Pam's ex. From what she's told me, he's a deeply unpleasant man. And before you say it, there's no danger of him coming here. Pam's got a restraining order. He's not allowed within a mile of her address."

"Well, if it was him who planted that bag of organs, he's already broken that, hasn't he?" They argued a little more, until Jess pulled him into the bedroom and began to undress. It seemed to resolve the issue.

Chapter Seven

The Yeardsley Trust was located in a small industrial estate on the outskirts of the city. It was purpose-built and had both workshop and office space. It offered opportunities for training and work experience for adults recovering from mental illness or with ongoing mental health issues, as well as people with learning difficulties and disabilities. The cynic in Neal noted that attendance at the Trust was linked to the receipt of benefits.

Megan Black, the Trust's manager, greeted Neal and Ava and ushered them into her office. She was a stout, fortyish woman, with voluminous black hair that reached to her waist. She was draped in loose-fitting garments in marbled shades of blue and grey, and she evidently had a fondness for chunky, arty jewellery. For all that she seemed larger than life, Megan Black was surprisingly softly spoken.

She invited Neal and Ava to sit down. "Terrible business. Leanne was a lovely young woman, everyone respected her. She'll be greatly missed."

Neal wondered how much contact Megan had had with Leanne. A lot of managers he'd come across had little to do with the admin staff in their organisation. "How well did you know Leanne?"

"Not that well, personally," Megan confessed. "But I heard glowing accounts of her from her line manager. I encouraged her to enrol in a part-time accounting course at Stromford College. She was a very capable person. She'd have moved on from here eventually, I suppose."

"Were you aware of Leanne's background when you took her on?" asked Neal.

"You mean the fact that she served time in prison, or the fact that she suffered emotional and quite possibly physical neglect as a child, Inspector?"

"Both. And you've just answered my question."

"I'm a great believer in second chances. Though 'second chance' is a bit of a misnomer when a person never had a chance in the first place, don't you think?"

Neal smiled. He recognised a kindred spirit in Megan Black.

"What exactly was Leanne's role here?"

"You'd probably be better off speaking to her supervisor about that. I'll take you down and introduce you."

The admin office was a box-shaped room with windows overlooking the car park. There were only five desks, one on its own, the others arranged in a group. Neal noticed a name plaque on one of these. Leanne Jackson. From the desk adjacent to Leanne's, a young woman smiled at Megan. Her eyes darted from Neal to Ava and back again.

"Good morning, Natalie." Megan looked towards the empty desks. "Where is everyone?"

"Beth's doing the post. Jack's dealing with an IT issue up in the Business Centre and Bryony's just nipped out to the toilet. Been ten minutes already, so she shouldn't be much longer."

"Please could you ask DI Neal and DS Merry if they'd like a drink while they wait for her?" Megan asked. Natalie took their orders and disappeared through a door, leading, presumably to the kitchen.

"Natalie's our apprentice," Megan whispered. "She's a bit inexperienced but she's a bright girl. Now, I'm sorry to rush away but I have to be at a meeting on the other side of Stromford in half an hour. Please get in touch if you want any more information about the Trust. I'm sure Bryony will be able to answer most of your questions when she arrives." And with that she left.

Ava crossed to Leanne's desk. There were no personal effects. Either there never had been or they had been removed already. She opened the desk drawers one by one to reveal the sort of items you'd expect to find in any office drawer: a ball of elastic bands, paper clips, a stapler, scissors . . .

"All exceptionally tidy and organised, just like PJ said her house was," Ava remarked. "Natalie could do with following her example." The apprentice's desk was cluttered with personal possessions. Ava picked up a pen with fluffy pink feathers attached to the top. "Remind you of anyone?"

Neal smiled, picturing PJ.

Natalie brought their drinks and by then Bryony had returned, closely followed by Beth and Jack.

"You must be the police officers Megan said were coming this morning to talk about Leanne. I'm Bryony Stamford, office manager." She dragged over a couple of chairs for Neal and Ava. "Terrible tragedy."

"It must have been a shock for everyone," Neal said. "How long had Leanne been with the Trust?"

"Just under a year. She was a good worker. Quick learner. I think she appreciated being given a chance to prove what she could do." Her eyes flicked to Natalie, and Neal gave a slight nod.

"What were Leanne's duties here, Ms Stamford?"

"She did general admin duties to begin with, and she proved so competent that I started giving her more complex tasks. She was wonderfully organised. She was always making suggestions to help streamline our procedures here." Bryony sighed. "She's going to be very hard to replace."

Neal nodded. "How well did you know Leanne on a personal level?"

"Not that well. None of us did, really. Leanne was a very private person. She joined in all the staff social activities — you know, birthdays and Christmas meals, but I wouldn't say she was great friends with anyone here. Certainly not with me, although we got on well enough as colleagues. I'm quite a bit older than Leanne was, married with kids. We didn't have a lot in common really."

"Natalie?" Neal turned to the girl, who had been hanging on their every word.

"I haven't been here long. I mostly talked to Leanne about work. We weren't friends or anything and she didn't talk about her personal life much." Natalie spoke hurriedly. Nerves, Neal guessed. Just as he thought she'd finished, she added, "I think she was having boyfriend problems, though. Someone called Seth. I heard her on the phone to him once. She called him a bastard and she sounded pretty upset." She gave a sideways look at Bryony. "I couldn't help overhearing."

But it wasn't Natalie's nosiness that was bothering Bryony. "Seth Conway?" she asked, sharply.

"I don't know his surname."

"You've heard of him?" Neal asked Bryony.

"If it's the same person, he did a placement here some time ago. He was a mental health nursing student. That was before Leanne came to work here, though."

Neal raised an eyebrow. "Did I pick up a hint that you disliked Seth Conway?

"You did, Inspector. Though I was pretty much alone in that. He had most people wrapped around round his little finger. Myself included, until I saw a completely different side to him, quite by chance."

"And that was . . .?"

"I saw him outside a club in town one night. Jeffers. Do you know it? On West Irongate Street?" Neal looked blank. Ava nodded.

"He was with a young girl. I know it's hard to tell these days, but I have a thirteen-year-old daughter and I don't think that girl was much older. I saw him give her a slap and pull her along by the hair. I was really shocked."

"Did you intervene?"

"My husband called out, but by the time we crossed the street and reached the door of the club, Seth had disappeared back inside."

"What about the girl?"

"He left her there. We offered to pay for a taxi to take her home but she refused. She said she had friends inside the club and she went back in to join them."

"Did you tell anyone about what you'd seen?"

Bryony looked shamefaced. "I spoke with Seth the Monday after it happened and he said I must have mistaken him for someone else."

"Could you have?"

"I suppose it's possible. I'm a bit short-sighted and I didn't have my contacts in. Seth left the Trust about a week after that, so I let it go."

"Do you remember the date when this incident occurred?" Neal asked.

Bryony nodded. "That's easy. It was my wedding anniversary." She gave them the date.

"I'd be grateful if you could let us know Seth Conway's contact details, Ms Stamford. It would save us a bit of time tracking him down. And a photograph would be useful."

"No problem. I'll ask Helen. She's our HR person." Bryony made the call and scribbled the details on a post-it.

Neal handed Bryony a copy of the list of names that had been found in Leanne's home, with the word 'victims' erased. "Do you recognise any of these names, Ms

Stamford? We thought it might be something that Leanne was working on for the Trust."

Bryony studied the list. "No, I don't think so. Actually, wait, two of the names are familiar. Chantelle Clarke. She was one of our clients. Sadly, she's no longer with us." Bryony lowered her voice. "She took her own life."

Neal nodded. "Yes, we were aware of the tragedy. And the other name you recognised?"

Bryony looked a little distressed. "Michaela Howard. Hers was another tragedy, I'm afraid. Oh dear, it's going to look as if all our clients meet some terrible fate after leaving here. It happens from time to time, of course, given that a lot of our attendees have mental health issues . . . Michaela drowned trying to rescue a dog. It was somewhere in Nottinghamshire, I think."

Neal nodded. "And the other three names, they don't mean anything to you?"

"I'll check our database, but the names aren't familiar."

"Thank you."

Bryony turned to her computer. "Ruby Kennedy, Alyssa Ballard and Corinna Masters never attended the Trust." She looked thoughtful. "I wonder. I'd tasked Leanne with creating a database of information on our former clients. We needed to know what happened to them after they left the Trust, for funding purposes mainly. Leanne was finding out how many had gone on to find work or apprenticeships, or secured a place at college. She volunteered to do it. It was just the sort of thing she was good at. I wonder if that's where she came across Chantelle Clarke and Michaela Howard. I'm not sure why she'd have written their names down at home though."

"How far had she progressed with this work?"

"She'd made good progress. I know she had quite a lot of difficulty tracking some of our former attendees down. She had to be a bit of a detective." She glanced sideways at Neal.

He smiled. "I'd be grateful if you would let us have access to the rest of the spreadsheet Leanne was working on." Seeing Bryony hesitate, he added, "Disclosure of information is permitted when it is required for the prevention and detection of crime and for the apprehension or prosecution of offenders."

Bryony frowned. "Oh, that should be okay then, but I'd still like to run it past Megan."

"I'd be grateful if you'd do that as soon as possible." Neal guessed there would be little of note in the spreadsheet, but it would be worth checking out the names against their own databases.

"Is there anything you can tell us about Leanne in the weeks leading up to her death? Did she say or do anything that was out of character, perhaps? Was she worrying about something?"

Bryony shook her head. "Not that I can think of."

At this, Beth Upton gave a sob. She and Jack had been largely silent, merely nodding or shaking their heads. Of all of them, Beth seemed the most upset over Leanne's death. Neal thought she was holding something back.

But Beth remained silent. It was Natalie who brought up the elephant in the room.

"Are they all dead too?" she asked, pointing to the other three names on Leanne's list.

"Natalie!" Bryony said sternly, but had probably been wondering the same thing.

"We don't even know who they are," Neal answered truthfully. "Maybe they're just people Leanne knew." The word 'victims' flashed into his mind.

"She knew a lot of dead people and now she's dead too," Natalie said, unhelpfully.

Neal was beginning to have a bad feeling about the other women on Leanne's list. From the way Ava's eyes lingered on the names, he could tell she was thinking the same.

"Thanks for your input everyone."

Ava was looking longingly at a cafetière on one of the worktops. It was the first sign she'd given that she was feeling hungover. It was hardly surprising, given how drunk she'd been the night before. It explained why she'd been taking a back seat all morning.

"There should be CCTV footage of the incident with Seth and the girl outside the nightclub," Neal remarked when they were back outside the Trust. "With luck we can find out who she is."

Ava was unusually quiet on the drive back to the station. Was she embarrassed about her behaviour the night before? She dropped Neal at the entrance to the station, though normally he came with her into the car park.

As soon as Neal walked in, Tom Knight stood up and came across. "We think we've got some information on one of the other names on Leanne's list, sir." PJ hovered by his side, looking like the cat that got the cream.

"Let's wait for DS Merry," Neal said. "My office in five."

In exactly five minutes, all four were sitting around Neal's desk. PJ had coffee for Ava and she poured iced tea for the others. It was her latest fad, according to Ava. Neal approved. He filled the others in on their visit to the Yeardsley Trust.

"So, what have you got?" Neal asked.

"Ruby Kennedy, sir."

Neal leaned forward. "Details?"

"Database came up with a match, sir. Her parents reported her missing some time ago. Ruby had been living with foster parents in another county until she was eighteen, then she took off on her own without telling anyone where she was going. Had a history of running away, apparently."

Neal nodded. "Have you checked out the other names on Leanne's list?"

"No match for any of the others, sir."

"Well, we have to assume that their names were there for a reason." Neal looked around. "Speculation?" It was something he often said when he wanted to encourage his team to share their thoughts.

"She knew them?" Ava suggested.

Neal smiled inwardly. Ava's still not firing on all cylinders, he thought.

Tom Knight shrugged. "You said Leanne had been working on compiling a database of the Trust's previous attendees. These names could simply be the ones she's been unable to follow up on."

Neal shook his head. "Bryony Stamford told us that none of these other women ever attended the Trust. We need to check the electoral lists and see if we can come up with matches for Alyssa Ballard and Corinna Masters. Get someone to look on social media sites too." He turned to Tom. "How was the interview with Leanne's next of kin?"

Tom told them.

"I'm interested in this anger management therapy group that Leanne attended and in the abusive boyfriend, although he's unlikely to be a factor after so long," said Neal. "Make sure you follow up on both these elements. And I want Chantelle's suicide and Michaela's drowning accident reviewed. We need to establish beyond a doubt that there were no suspicious circumstances."

"OK, chief."

Ava was looking pensive. "Strange. Leanne would have known that Michaela Howard and Chantelle Clarke were dead, but not Ruby Kennedy, as far as we're aware. Leanne included Ruby in her list of so-called 'victims,' but Ruby must have been alive when she compiled the list. Sorry to be gruesome, but if it wasn't a death list, what exactly did Leanne consider them to be victims of?"

"Or who?" PJ gave a shiver. "What's that saying? One's coincidence, two's chance, three's a pattern." A grim silence followed her words.

Neal tilted his head. "Maybe yes, maybe no. We need to do the groundwork before we make any inferences. We must find the other two women on the list for one thing." He looked from Tom to PJ. "Make that a priority. If either of those women is missing, someone may be holding them captive somewhere — or worse. Worst case scenario? We could be looking at two more deaths."

Chapter Eight

As though they'd summoned her from the netherworld, Ruby Kennedy's body turned up the following day. Neal informed his team in sombre mood, and asked Ava to accompany him to the scene.

Ruby's body had been discovered on a secluded stretch of the River Strom, where it meandered through sporadic woodland near the village of Carlby, some ten miles from the centre of Stromford. Summer foliage and a steep embankment had hidden it from sight. Neal, Ashley and Ava arrived to find a couple of uniformed officers waiting with a huddle of community volunteers in yellow jackets with 'Stromford River Trust' emblazoned across their backs.

Neal greeted one of the PCs, who introduced himself as Bill Purdy.

A middle-aged woman stepped forward. "I'm Norma Standish. I coordinate the volunteer activities in this part of the county." She led them to the edge of the embankment. The victim was lying on the riverbank just clear of the water. "Two of us clambered down the embankment to see if she was breathing, even though it was pretty obvious she wasn't going to be, poor lass." Norma grimaced. "We lifted her clear of the water. We couldn't just leave here there. I'm sorry if that was the wrong thing to do, forensically speaking." No one told Norma she'd been wrong.

Norma was the sort of no-nonsense person Neal liked to deal with at a murder scene. No histrionics, just a concise account of the discovery of the body. He looked at Ashley, who was already suiting up.

"Let's take a look, shall we?" the pathologist said, wearily. Neal and Ava slithered down the steep embankment after him. Ava held some low hanging tree branches aside, and Ashley bent low over the young woman to feel her neck for a pulse and make a short examination.

"What are you thinking, Ash?" Neal asked.

"You don't need me to tell you she's been in the water for a while," Ash said. Neal nodded. The corpse was bloated, the stomach distended and there was maceration or wrinkling of the skin on the hands and feet. It was also blotched with patches of green and black, like bruises. Lividity. Neal frowned. Ash read his mind, "At a glance, pattern of blood pooling isn't typical of drowning. Would expect to see more in the head and neck, which leads me to suspect death occurred on land."

Neal knew this conclusion was based on a cursory examination, and wasn't definitive. Even so, Ash had been in this game so long that even his guesses were probably right.

"Look at the head." Neal looked, and thought he understood what Ash was getting at.

"The position? Turned to the side?"

Ash nodded. "Again, not typical of a drowning."

"Anything else?"

"Not yet. Sorry, Jim. Ante-mortem injuries are going to be hard to detect, given the extent of putrefaction."

Ashley cast a look of lingering sadness on the young woman, as did Neal. Of the three of them, childless Ava seemed the least affected by the sight. Neal suspected that his sergeant was still a long way from considering motherhood. He thought of Myrna in the weeks leading up to their son Archie's birth — her slow, cumbersome movements and aching back. Neal suspected that, for Ava, the worst aspect of pregnancy would be the vulnerability. She wouldn't willingly give up her physical prowess.

Ava was looking around. "This isn't a particularly busy area. We'll be lucky if a witness comes forward. It is Ruby, isn't it?

"I think so," Neal said. Despite the condition of the body, it was still possible to discern something of the girl's features.

They climbed back up the embankment, where more police officers and SOCOs had joined the sombre group of volunteers.

Chapter Nine

Ever since the 'organ incident' as they called it now, Jess had been jumpy. Like the policeman, she thought the perpetrator was most likely Pam's ex, Michael Hollings. That meant Hollings might be capable of worse. Pam had told Jess she left Michael after only two years of marriage because of his unreasonable behaviour. She hadn't said as much, but Jess suspected that physical violence might have been a factor. Unreasonable people had a tendency to become even more unreasonable when they didn't get their own way.

"Marry in haste, repent at leisure. The old adage is true, at least in my case," Pam had said to her. "I was still grieving for my lovely Stan and afraid of facing a future on my own. Michael came along out of the blue and proposed after only six weeks. I thought, 'Why the hell not?' I didn't have time to find out what a possessive bastard he was. It was the usual thing — gradually becoming isolated because Michael was jealous of my friendships, staying at home more and more because he didn't like me going out. I wasn't going to hang about waiting for the next slap. I'm afraid I was a classic case."

"No you weren't," Jess reassured her. "You realised your mistake and got out. You hear so many stories of women staying in abusive relationships for years."

"I'd never thought of myself as a victim. Fortunately it didn't take me too long to come to my senses and realise what kind of man Michael really was." She sighed. "I just want the divorce over and done with so I can get on with my life."

"You're doing that already." Jess counted herself lucky to have ended up with Pam as a neighbour, and she had come to value Pam's advice. But she certainly wasn't going to sit back and 'let the police do their job' in the case of Leanne's death. Her conversation with DS Ava Merry at the pool had been deeply disappointing. She appreciated that Ava couldn't divulge any details of an ongoing investigation, but she'd hoped to hear something to reassure her that the police were making progress.

Mitch was being more attentive than ever since the offal incident. After the news of Leanne's murder, he even suggested she avoid walking alone after dark. Jess teased him about his over-protective attitude, but she also quite liked it. Mitch's job reflected his protective personality. It was in his nature to be caring, she knew, but Pam's experience had taught her to be wary of controlling men. It certainly wouldn't be a good idea to let Mitch know that she intended to look into Leanne's death herself.

It was half past two in the afternoon, but Jess had already finished for the day. She walked into town. The aroma of freshly brewed coffee from a café on the High Street enticed her inside. She was feeling deflated, and a couple of shots of caffeine would perk her up. She stood at the counter, fumbling with her purse, and a hand reached across her, holding out a ten pound note.

"My treat, and can I get an Americano. Extra shot, please.'

"Jonty?"

"Hi, Jess. I saw you come in and thought I'd join you. I hope you don't mind. There's a couple of things I wanted to ask you to do with Barney."

Did she mind? Jess wasn't sure. He'd given her no opportunity to refuse. He led the way to a table by the window.

"I see there's no news yet," he said. Jess frowned. "About your friend? There's been nothing on the news about how the investigation's going."

"No. I'm sure they're doing everything they can." Jess thought of DS Merry and their meeting at the pool.

"Yes. I'm sure it's only a matter of time before they get someone for it."

Jess nodded. She gazed out the window at a smoker at a table outside, just a pane of glass away. She remembered walking past the woods at the end of the school playing field once and seeing Leanne standing alone, smoking. She smiled at Jess and held out her packet of cigarettes, but Jess shook her head and hurried on. Why hadn't she stopped? She looked back at Jonty. "Yes, I expect so."

"You look sad," he said.

"Do I?"

"Are you still upset about her?"

Of course I am. Jess blew on her coffee, hoping it would cool quickly so that she could drink it quickly and go.

"When did you last see her?"

Hadn't she told him that morning on the bridge? Why did he want to know, anyway? It was none of his business. *Come on,* she told herself, *he is only being friendly.* Was she treating him as she had treated Leanne that day by the woods? Or was she simply twisting everything to fit her image of herself as someone no one really wanted to befriend or love?

"Sorry," Jonty said. "I wasn't being nosey. I was just going to say that you should focus on the last time you saw her when she was happy. Remember her that way. That's what everyone told me when my gran died. She had dementia, and I try not to think of how she was in her last few months, but of how kind she was to me and Barney when we were kids."

The last time she had seen Leanne? Being dragged through the town centre by a couple of PCs, drunk and kicking. Nice last image to focus on.

"Thanks, Jonty. That's good advice. I'm sorry about your gran." *Be nice,* she told herself. For the next twenty minutes, Jess concentrated on having a conversation with Jonty, and to her surprise, she found herself liking him. Jonty talked about Barney a lot. Rather too much, Jess thought. Was he using Barney to cast himself in a favourable light? Still, it *was* admirable that he cared so much for his brother.

After a while, Jess stood up to go. Jonty looked up at her shyly. "I . . . er . . . I don't suppose you'd like to go out sometime?"

Jess cleared her throat. "Actually, I'm seeing someone."

Jonty gave an embarrassed laugh. "Well, he's a lucky guy. If it doesn't work out between you, keep me in mind, won't you?"

Oh God. Jess would have to be honest. "Listen, Jonty, you're a lovely bloke, but . . . I just don't think . . ."

"Sorry, Jess. I've put you in a really awkward position. I do understand." He gave her a shy smile. "Friends?"

Jess hesitated, then smiled. "Friends."

It was only after she left the café that she realised Jonty hadn't even mentioned the 'couple of things' concerning Barney.

Yet again, Jess's thoughts turned to Leanne.

That day in the corridor near the art room, when she had stuck up for Jess, Leanne had been so fearless. It occurred to Jess that Leanne could have been popular if she'd put her mind to it. She was pretty and clever enough to get in with the cool kids. But she'd remained on the outside, a lone wolf. Was it out of choice? Leanne had been in prison. She seemed to have turned her life around since coming out. But what if she'd gone off the rails again, and got herself mixed up in something bad? It wasn't what Jess wanted to believe. She wanted to believe Leanne had got herself killed because she'd used that same courage and fearlessness to help someone else.

By the time four o'clock arrived, a thin headache was threading its way through Jess's skull, the onset of a migraine perhaps or a sign that she needed some rest. Instead she went home and stilled her mind in a burst of cleaning.

Returning the vacuum cleaner to its stand in the hall, she noticed an envelope sticking through her letterbox and tugged it out. There was nothing on the front or back — no address, no stamp. She tucked it under her arm and went off to the kitchen to make tea. As she waited for the kettle to boil, she tore open the envelope and extracted a folded sheet of paper. A single sentence was printed there in a bold gothic font.

"Stop looking into things that don't concern you or people close to you could get hurt."

The note fluttered to the floor. Jess looked around her small kitchen. All the familiar knickknacks suddenly seemed less homely. Even the yellow smiley stickers on her calendar, marking the days when she'd stuck to her alcohol limit, seemed to grin at her with a sense of menace. She returned to the hall to double check that she had locked her door. Her key was still in the lock, and she twisted it out and hung it on the hook above the radiator.

Back in the kitchen, Jess picked the note up with the prongs that she used for turning meat under the grill. She knew it was important not to contaminate evidence, and she intended to show the letter to DS Ava Merry first thing in the morning. Before she could place it somewhere for safekeeping, she was interrupted by an urgent knocking on her door.

She opened it and gasped. Pam stood on the mat outside. She had a cut on her forehead and the beginnings of a black eye. "What happened to you?"

"I was bloody mugged. In broad daylight. On my way back from the cinema. A man grabbed me from behind and demanded some money. Luckily I didn't have much cash on me, but he took my mobile phone." Pam's voice was shrill with hysteria. Jess thought of the note.

"Oh, Pam!"

"It was all over so quickly. One minute I was walking along minding my own business, the next I felt my arm being grabbed and I was pushed against a wall."

Jess put her arm round Pam's shoulder. "He . . . he didn't have a knife or anything, did he, Pam?"

"No. But it was still pretty scary."

"I'll bet. Pity you didn't have Bunty with you. Not that she's much good as a guard dog, but seeing her might have deterred him."

"She would have licked him to death." They both smiled.

"Are you going to report the incident to the police?"

"Probably not much point, but I suppose I should. I'm afraid I can't give them much of a description though. He was wearing a hoodie — of course — and he twisted my arm behind my back so I couldn't turn around to get a look at his face."

"I'll go down to the station with you now, if you like."

Pam gave a reluctant nod. "Do you mind if Bunty comes along?"

"Give me your keys and I'll go and fetch her. I'll be right back." Jess ran off, and they were soon fussing over Bunty.

"I'm so glad I've got her. I couldn't bear to be alone in my flat tonight."

"I could stay over if you like?" Jess offered immediately.

"Oh no. There's no need. Bunty will look after me, won't you, darling dog?"

The desk officer at the station eyed Pam's wounds with a look of concern.

"We've come to report a crime," Jess explained. "My friend's been mugged."

The officer asked Pam if she required victim support, which she declined. He sounded apologetic, but couldn't offer much else. "It's unlikely that the perpetrator will be caught. There were no witnesses, we don't have much of a description and he only took a little bit of cash and your phone."

"Only." Pam sighed.

"I expect you're really busy now with the murder investigation?" Jess said. Pam stared at her, while the officer merely nodded.

"I was on the bridge over the river the morning after, when the frogmen were searching the river. There were a lot of police there too. Do you know if they have any leads?"

The officer's look became suspicious. "You from the Courier?"

"No. It's just . . . oh, never mind. I'm just interested, that's all. It's not every day you see something like that. There aren't many murders in Stromford."

"You'd be surprised," the officer muttered. He asked a few more questions, and asked Pam if her husband could have put someone up to mugging her. Jess had already considered this, but Pam seemed appalled.

Soon they were back outside. "Well, that was a waste of time," declared Pam. "Michael's a shit but he wouldn't go that far."

"Well, at least the police have it on their books in case anything else happens," Jess said. She fingered the letter in her jacket pocket. Was this what Mitch called an 'escalation?' She should go back inside and show it to the desk officer. But Pam was still looking shaken from her experience and there seemed no point in upsetting her further. Jess stuffed the note deeper into her pocket and said nothing.

When Mitch came round that evening, Jess told him about the mugging. It was all she could do to talk him out of stomping upstairs to ask Pam for Michael's address.

"We don't even know he had anything to do with it."

"Come off it, Jess. Who else could it be? He's got someone to rough her up a bit, give her a fright. He was a controlling bastard, wasn't he? Didn't want her to leave him. I know the type — well, not personally, but you know what I mean." Mitch liked reading books about true crimes. Jess suspected he read them for the gruesome parts.

Mitch was moody for the rest of the evening and Jess wished she hadn't said anything. Knowing how protective he was, she had expected him to be angry with whoever did it, then supportive. Instead he sat in stony silence all through their meal. When they sat down to watch TV and she sidled up to him on the sofa, he pushed her away. Finally, he revealed the true reason for his mood.

"Luke saw you in Costa this afternoon." Luke was one of Mitch's firemen buddies. "You were with someone."

"Jonty Cole. He's the brother of one of my students, Barney. He wanted to talk to me about him."

"So why couldn't he do that at college? "

"I don't know. Maybe he happened to see me in town and it came into his mind."

"Right."

"What is this, Mitch? We only had coffee and a quick chat."

"Oh, yeah. About Barney, right?"

Jess felt her hackles rise. "Yes, about Barney." Mitch stared at the television for the next ten minutes without saying a word. Jess stared too, angry. She was angry at Mitch for acting like a jealous schoolboy, angry at herself, but mostly she was just seething with an incoherent rage that would not be stilled, however hard she stared at the screen. Finally, she erupted.

She stood up and nodded at the door. "I'd like you to leave." She couldn't make out Mitch's expression. Was it astonishment? Bewilderment? Jess didn't care. "Get out."

"Jess?"

"I don't want any discussion. Just go."

Mitch gathered his things together and left without another word. He didn't slam the door and this for some reason made Jess feel all the angrier.

Chapter Ten

Jonty's rage still simmered. He kept thinking about his encounter with Jess, going over and over it in his mind. What had she said? 'You're a really nice guy, Jonty, but I'm seeing someone.' Inferring that if she hadn't been seeing anyone, she still wouldn't touch him with a barge pole. At least the boyfriend part wasn't a lie to put him off. He'd seen them together. A guy called Mitch. A fireman.

I held it together well, didn't I? he thought. Smiled and even managed to mouth some bullshit about Mitch being a lucky guy. Well, he'd given the bitch a chance and she'd blown it. Whatever feelings he'd had for her were gone now, blasted away by her rejection. In a way, he was relieved. It felt like a weight had been lifted off his shoulders. Love, or whatever it was he'd felt for Jess, was gone. Killing her would be easy now.

But he'd take his time.

It was too soon after the others. Victims were like buses it seemed, they always came in threes. Jonty felt like laughing. The memory of the Jackson bitch rising like Lazarus from the dead came back to him. And then she'd thrown herself into the river, right in the middle of town.

He'd been up on deck steering the boat, and the din of music booming from the bars on the waterfront was the only sound he'd heard.

She'd chosen her spot alright. Lucky for him, no one had seen the bitch go over the side. And she'd taken the iron he'd used to finish her. Shit. He'd been so sure she was dead. Anyway, it had taught him never to be so careless again.

It had been a risky but necessary undertaking kidnapping her and the Kennedy girl at the same time. Keeping them both on the boat together had also been taking a chance. The plan had been to cruise the waterways until he found the right place to dispose of them. And to enjoy beating them until he got there. He hadn't expected Leanne to fight back so hard. She'd been like a fucking Ninja. He still bore the bruises from her kicks. But she'd been no match for him in the end.

The Kennedy girl had been different. He'd made sure she was bound up tight before he laid into her. Less of a challenge, but he needed to finish her off quickly. If the police ever linked her with Leanne, he didn't want them finding her on his boat.

He'd chosen a stretch of river that was secluded and weighted her pockets with bricks, knowing she'd float eventually. And now she had. It was on the news this morning. The police were bound to make the connection with Leanne.

Jonty broke his own rule and got in touch with Seth Conway. They met in a quiet park, but even so, Conway had been a fucking wreck. He was as nervous as Jonty about being seen together. The irony of it. A murderer and a paedophile, and neither wanted anything to do with the other.

"You didn't have to kill them." Seth, head in hands, crying like a baby.

Jonty stared at him. "What? You were happy to go to prison?"

"I was going to leave the country."

Jonty couldn't believe what he was hearing. A combination of luck and charm had saved Seth's skin in the past, but this time things were different. Leanne had been like a terrier with a rat between her teeth. She'd got the Kennedy girl on her side, and who knows how many of the other girls she'd have persuaded to testify if he hadn't stopped her.

"You came to me with this problem, remember? What did you think I was going to do? Talk to them about it? *Counsel* them?" Jonty brought his face close to Seth's. "You threatened me, Seth. You said, 'If I go down, I take you with me.' Tell me that wasn't your cowardly way of asking me to take care of Leanne Jackson and the Kennedy girl." Silence. "Thought so."

"What about the others?" Seth muttered. "The others in that group, back then?"

"Even if Leanne managed to contact them, they won't talk now that she's dead. All you have to do is keep your head down for a bit. No more parties until I say so. The last thing you need is to be picked up on some underage sex charge and have your DNA and fingerprints setting off fireworks in the police databases."

Neither of them mentioned that other girl, but her death hung in the air between them. The one Seth hadn't been able to help after Jonty finished with her. Sasha: fifteen years old, and on the game. No one missed her dead any more than they'd noticed her when she was alive. Jonty smiled at the memory. She'd been no beauty, but the way she screamed when Jonty punched her again and again was truly ravishing. Who needed beauty? None of them looked pretty when he'd finished with them. They were just meat — red, raw and ugly.

Afterwards, Seth had punched her some more, in a pathetic attempt to restart her heart. When it refused to beat, he had gone to pieces. So, invigorated by the kill, Jonty assumed control. He cleaned up, disposed of the body, and even calmed Seth down, eventually. Not before Seth had muttered that he was through with Jonty, finished with putting girls his way to feed his 'monstrous, sick appetite.' Jonty couldn't stop laughing at the absurdity of this — Seth assuming he occupied the higher moral ground.

"You think you're better than me?"

"I've never killed anyone. I treat those girls well. Better than their families ever did. I love them."

"Love?" Now this really was a joke. Jonty knew something about the way paedos think. Seth genuinely believed he wasn't harming his victims. He told Jonty once that he'd chosen to be a nurse because he loved children. Not a hint of irony. Seth really believed the evil monster inside him was nothing but a fluffy bunny rabbit.

Jonty, on the other hand, had no illusions about himself. He knew very well that he was a twisted and evil being that fed on the pain of others. There was a word for it but Jonty didn't care for labels. He regarded himself as unique. He wasn't just another psychopath whose traits could be listed as typical in some student's textbook.

This whole business with Jackson and Kennedy had made Jonty wonder if Seth's usefulness to him was worth the risk. He panicked and disposed of their bodies carelessly. Not Jonty. He doubted anyone would ever go looking for Sasha, but if they did, they'd find it hard. Only Seth could reveal her whereabouts. That was why Jonty listened when Seth threatened to take him down. Why he'd had to help him. Jonty knew that one of these days, he would have to deal with Seth once and for all.

Chapter Eleven

A couple of days after their visit to the Yeardsley Trust, Ava received a message from Beth Upton asking if they could meet. She suggested a café in a garden centre well away from town, the sort of place you might choose if you didn't want to be seen by your work colleagues.

The traffic was horrendous, and Ava was late getting there. Beth was sitting at a table inside, looking out towards the lake. She had evidently chosen this table because from where she was sitting, she had a clear view of both entrances. She looked up when Ava walked in.

Ava slid into the seat across from her. "Nice to see you again, Beth."

"Thanks for meeting me. I didn't feel I could talk freely at the office with everyone listening." Beth's eyes darted around the room. They were the only customers sitting inside. It was busy enough outside, where a number of silver-haired customers were enjoying the sunshine and the antics of the ducks waddling around on the decking.

Ava waited, watching an array of expressions flit over Beth's face. Whatever she had to say, it was causing her some internal conflict.

"What do you know about Leanne's background?" she asked at last.

"Are you referring to the fact that she'd been in prison?"

"Actually, no. I knew about that, of course. Bryony never mentioned it, but Stromford's a small town. That kind of thing gets around. My husband grew up on the same estate as Leanne. Her family had a bad rep and it was common knowledge that Leanne ended up in prison. That, and the fact that her case was in the court reports in the Courier at the time. Paul, my husband, remembers reading about it. It was the first thing he said when I mentioned the name of my new colleague at work."

"Why did you ask what I knew about Leanne's early life?"

"I just wanted to know that you aren't making the wrong assumptions."

"In what way?"

"You know, assuming that she was into something illegal that might have got her killed. Because I'm pretty sure she wasn't. In fact, I think Leanne was killed because she was investigating something illegal."

Ava nodded, impressed. Beth was cleverer than she seemed. Ava had learned to be patient, to wait. People who wanted to talk would get around to it in their own time. Still, she couldn't resist a little prompt. "Did Leanne confide something in you, Beth?"

Beth's bottom lip trembled and her words poured out in a rush. "Yes. She was afraid. She believed that she was going to die. She thought Seth Conway was going to kill her."

Ava hadn't expected this. "Leanne told you that?"

"Not in those exact words."

"What did she say?" Ava leaned forward.

"She said that if anything happened to her, I should contact the police and tell them about what she'd been investigating." Ava held her breath. "I didn't want to mention anything in front of Bryony because Leanne told me this one day when I saw her in town. She was on a day off but, er, I was on a . . . a sick day." Ava nodded, understanding that she'd lied about the sickness. She didn't speak up at work because she feared she'd get into trouble.

"Did Leanne tell you what she'd been investigating, Beth? Did she give you any details?"

"I—"

"Bacon butty, lettuce, no mustard?" The waitress placed Ava's order in front of her. "Enjoy." Talk about bad timing.

"Beth?"

"No. She was going to tell me but she got too upset to speak. I was supposed to be going round to her place after the weekend, but . . ."

But in the meantime, Leanne's fears had been realised. Ava tore at her butty. Always the same. One step forward, two steps back.

"I'm sorry. I should have told you sooner. I was hoping you'd investigate Seth Conway after what Bryony said about him mistreating that girl, but then I kept thinking, what if you didn't? Supposing Seth did kill Leanne and he got away with it because I didn't speak up?"

Ava swallowed. "Please don't apologise. Natalie told us Leanne might have been seeing Seth, so we are looking into him."

Beth frowned. "Between you and me, I wouldn't believe everything Natalie says. We've caught her out on a few whoppers. When she started working at the Trust, she was always going on about her amazing boyfriend. It was all Sam this and Sam that. Honest to God you'd have thought the sun shone out of Sam's . . . well, you know what I mean. To cut a long story short, it turned out Sam was a figment of her imagination. And there was other stuff about where she'd been and what she'd done — all made up."

Ava nodded. Tracking down Seth Conway was proving to be tricky. The Trust had given them an address he'd never lived at.

They sat without speaking for a minute. Ava reached up to open a window and the sounds of the outside world drifted in, reminding her that there was more to life than just this case. She watched a pair of Egyptian ducks terrorising the other ducks at the lake's edge. It reminded her of a story Neal told her about Archie feeding the ducks in the park one day. He'd been upset at their aggressive behaviour and had chased them away from the breadcrumbs he'd been scattering. 'So unready for the world that is waiting for him,' Neal had said.

Beth was looking at her. "I hope I haven't wasted your time, Sergeant Merry."

Ava returned to the present. "Not at all. You've been very helpful."

"Is it alright if I go now?" Beth asked.

"Sure. Are you doing anything nice with the rest of your free afternoon?"

"I think I might just go home. I haven't been sleeping well since I heard about Leanne. Maybe I'll be able to relax, now that I've got this off my chest."

Ava watched Beth make her way to the side door. Suddenly her butty tasted of nothing at all.

* * *

"Success." Looking smug, PJ put the phone down.

"Michaela Howard?" Tom asked.

PJ nodded. "Just had confirmation from Notts police about her drowning."

Tom handed her another glass of iced tea and perched on the edge of her desk.

"Okay," PJ continued, "So Michaela Howard drowned trying to rescue a dog from the river, as Bryony Whatsit told Ava and the chief. The dog drowned too. A young lad witnessed the tragedy."

"Any other witnesses?"

"Nope."

"Was it Michaela's dog?"

"No, but it was chipped and the owners were traced. They claimed it had been missing for two days. Imagine how they must have felt when they learned it was the cause of a young woman's death."

"Was there an inquest?"

"Yes, the verdict was accidental death. But there were one or two anomalies. Michaela's parents claimed she was afraid of water and never learned to swim. Then again, she *was* a real animal lover. Her mother said she couldn't have passed a dog in distress without trying to rescue it."

Tom shook his head. "What sort of dumbass risks their life for a bloody dog?"

"Michaela had ADHD. Impulsive behaviour is a common symptom. She would probably have reacted without thinking."

"Shit. You should have told me that before."

Soon, Tom had tracked down another of the women. "Alyssa Ballard emigrated to Australia. I'll find her contact details and see if she can tell me anything about the other women on the list."

"So that only leaves Corinna Masters." PJ looked up. "Hey, Ava. How did your meeting with Beth Upton go?"

Before Ava had a chance to reply, Neal summoned the three of them into his office.

Neal rubbed at his eyes. "Right. Ruby Kennedy. Ash is as certain as he can be that she had extensive ante-mortem injuries. She was dead when she went into the water . . ." His voice tailed off.

"Any evidence of sexual assault, sir?" asked Ava.

"None." Neal picked up the copies of the report that had been lying on his desktop. The contents seemed to seep through the thin manila envelope and contaminate the very air. He gave them a few moments to read it.

"There is some good news. Forensics have found traces of DNA under Ruby's fingernails." Their faces brightened. "That's solid evidence. All we need to do now is find out who it belongs to. That's what we're good at, people, is it not?" He managed a thin-lipped smile.

"That's great, sir," Ava said immediately.

Neal looked at his colleagues. "So, what else do we have? Where are we with locating the other women on Leanne's list?"

Tom told him. "So, three out of four of the women whose names were highlighted on Leanne's list are known to be deceased. One committed suicide, one accidentally drowned, and one was brutally murdered. The fourth, Alyssa Ballard, is now living in Australia having emigrated five years ago and we're, er," Tom glanced at PJ, "working on establishing the whereabouts of Corinna Masters."

"Get in touch with Nottingham again and request a copy of the witness statement for Michaela's drowning. I'd like to review it and if possible speak with the SIO in charge of that case. I want to know if anyone involved in that investigation suspected foul play, or if anything about the incident didn't ring true."

"Yessir." Ava and PJ chorused.

"Ava, what did Beth Upton have to say?"

"Leanne was afraid of Seth Conway. She was convinced that he was going to kill her. I think we can now be certain that Leanne was killed because of something she'd discovered about these women, sir."

"I agree." Neal rubbed his chin. "I'm wondering if the names on Leanne's list may be women she knew personally. We need to build up a profile of each of these young women and find out what they had in common. We are looking for a link between them and Leanne. The most obvious one, of course, is that they all had mental health issues."

Tom made a face. "Our interview with Tina Jackson didn't yield much info. And from what Leanne's colleagues at the Trust said, she was a pretty private person. Even this Beth, who claims to have been a friend, doesn't seem to know a lot about her."

"There must have been someone she was close to," said PJ. "What about when she was in prison? And do we know much about what she did between her release from prison and getting the job at the Trust?"

Neal nodded. "These are all gaps that need to be filled in. Leanne's mother mentioned an anger management group. Tom, any luck on following that up?" Tom shook his head. "Contact CAMHS, the Child Adolescent Mental Health Service and obtain access to any records they may have on Leanne and the others. Get a warrant, if necessary. And see what we can find out about this abusive boyfriend Tina Jackson alluded to." Neal took a breath. "Okay, that's all for now. Back to work, everyone."

'Yessir!'

Chapter Twelve

Jess reached for Mitch's warm, familiar body but the sheets on his side of the bed were cold and empty. Then she remembered their row. She lay on her back, staring at the ceiling, wondering if this was the end of their relationship. She realised she was hoping it wasn't.

This disheartening start set a pattern for the rest of her day. She got to work and was sent off on a course that was unrelated to her job. She spent much of her morning staring out of the window, morbidly dissecting her relationship with Mitch. Was he too controlling, or had she really been raging at Leanne's killer?

Later, she drove to Tesco's to do some grocery shopping. There was a hint of summer in the air, and Jess began to feel more cheerful. She emerged from the supermarket and the day turned blacker still. Her front tyres were completely flat. She peered closer. Someone had slashed them with a knife. Then, when she went to unlock the car door she discovered that it was already open. She always checked at least twice that she'd locked it, and today had been no exception. Jess looked around nervously. The cars around her took on a sinister air as if any one of them could be harbouring a crazed tyre slasher ready to jump out on her with a knife. A meerkat in the back window of the car parked in front of her grinned menacingly.

Jess checked the back seat of the car. She opened the boot, slowly, warily. Everything looked normal. But her day was about to get even worse. Her phone rang. As soon as Pam spoke, Jess knew something was terribly wrong.

"Is that you, Jess? Oh, Jess, Bunty's gone missing."

Jess sat on the edge of the back seat. "Oh, Pam."

Pam sounded as if she was starting to hyperventilate.

Jess heard a man's voice in the background. "Pam?" she said, "Is someone with you?"

"Hello. Jess?" The voice was loud in her ear. "My name's Henry. I'm a friend of Pam's. I'm afraid she's too upset to speak at the moment."

"Please, just tell her to try not to worry. I can't come right now — my car's been vandalised and I can't move it. Tell her I'll see her as soon as I can." The man promised to relay her message. At least Pam wasn't alone.

Jess called the AA. She was beginning to get the jitters. First the grisly organ incident, then Pam's mugging and now this. Was it just a run of bad luck? Or was it something more? It was all very strange. Jess's first thought was that Mitch had slashed her tyres in an act of spite, then she felt ashamed for thinking so badly of him. Then she thought of Pam's ex, Michael Hollings, but that made no sense at all. They'd never even met. Then there was the anonymous note, the threat underpinning all the rest.

As she waited, Jess's fingers hovered over Ava's number. Then, reluctant to bother her again, she put her phone away.

The AA man advised her to report the matter to the police. Jess wasn't going to bother. She spoke to one of the security team at the store reception desk about the CCTV covering the area where she'd been parked. The camera was broken. Regrettably.

"It happens from time to time," the store manager said, apologetically. "Wanton vandalism. Can't understand what sort of kick a person gets out of it."

"You should get them fixed," Jess said, irritably.

"We'll keep a note of the incident," the manager assured her, "in case the police need to refer to it in the future."

By the time she was able to drive again, Jess was feeling utterly riled. She bought some flowers for Pam and drove slowly home.

When she finally knocked on Pam's door, Henry answered, and greeted her with a reassuring smile and a firm handshake. "I'm sorry to be meeting you for the first time on such an occasion."

"How is she?" Jess asked quietly.

"Bearing up well. If it had been my Boris, I'd be a quivering wreck. Pam is a very brave woman." Henry sounded slightly camp. He was lean and sharp-featured, a dapper, albeit slightly eccentric dresser. For some reason, Jess had been expecting a much older man. Henry didn't look a day over fifty.

"I'm fine." Pam appeared at her kitchen door accompanied by a dog that could only be Boris. "Henry and Boris have been looking after me."

"I'm so sorry, Pam. Have you told the police?"

Pam gave a little sniff. "Yes. Fat lot of good it did. They took down a description and said they'd contact the dog warden and ask her to look out for her. Henry and I have just got back from tying flyers to lampposts and distributing them around the local area." She looked shattered, and a tear rolled down her cheek. Jess gave her a hug. "And what about you?" Pam asked. "Henry told me you said something about your car being vandalised."

Jess explained about her tyres. Pam looked thoughtful. "I'm beginning to think that all these horrible things that have been happening this week are more than just coincidence." Jess said nothing. She didn't know how much Pam had told Henry of the week's events.

"What horrible things?" So he knew nothing. At a nod from Pam, Jess went ahead and told him. "But this is shocking," he declared. "Why didn't you tell me about all this, Pam? I wish I'd been there when that guy mugged you."

Pam touched his arm. "Bless you. It's probably just as well you weren't, though. You were bad enough when that boy threw a stone at Bunty. I thought you were going to throttle him."

"He would have deserved it," Henry replied. Pam squeezed the arm.

Jess handed Pam the flowers. "I got these for you. I'll just have a bite to eat, then I'll go out and look for Bunty. I'm sure Magda will too if she's not working."

"Bless you. Henry, Boris and I are going out again too, when we've had a little rest. Maybe Boris will be able to pick up Bunty's scent."

Jess went downstairs. As soon as she was inside her flat, she found herself making for the kitchen and the cupboard where she kept her glasses. She hadn't told Pam and Henry about the note she'd found — when? She pulled it from her pocket and the menacing words leapt out at her. She returned to the hallway and double checked that she'd locked the door. Someone had broken into her car. What was to stop them breaking into her home? She'd always thought people were being melodramatic when they said a break-in was a kind of violation. Now she thought she understood what they meant.

Tomorrow, she'd see again about having the locks changed, at least on the main entrance door. Jess ate a simple meal of pasta and salad and then grabbed her coat. She knocked on Magda's door but there was no answer. Magda worked as a care assistant and her hours were long and irregular.

Outside, Jess zipped up her thin jacket. It was that time of year between late Spring and early summer when the evening air can be chilly. Jess suspected it was as much nerves as cold that made her shivery. For the next hour and a half, she traipsed around the streets, covering all the routes that she normally walked with Bunty. Now and again she called out the dog's name.

Jess also searched the west common and told the dog walkers there about Bunty' disappearance. After two hours, she was thoroughly tired and disheartened. She looked at the grazing ponies. Had they seen a stray chocolate Labrador? The ponies grazed on.

As the light began to fade, Jess became tense and jumpy. She turned into her own street, and saw Pam, Henry and Boris coming towards her.

Pam grasped Jess's hand. "Thank you so much for looking for Bunty all this time. Henry, Boris and I are going to search again. I've given Boris one of Bunty's toys to help him catch her scent." Jess looked down and saw a grey fluffy rabbit hanging from Boris's mouth.

"I hope you find her," Jess said, without much hope. "Goodnight, everyone."

Inside her flat, Jess was still uneasy. Afraid of the gaping darkness behind the doors, she left lights on in every room. Twice she had to stop herself rechecking the locks on the outside door. She wondered if Henry would be staying the night at Pam's. She didn't like to think of her friend being alone, especially if they failed to find Bunty.

Unable to concentrate on reading or watching TV, Jess went to bed, but couldn't sleep. She lay awake, alert to the slightest noise. Around midnight she dozed off but woke again at one. At about one thirty she thought she heard the sound of the front door scraping open. Her first thought was that it might be Magda returning from a late shift. Then she remembered about Pam and Henry's search and sat up. She heard the door scrape shut again.

Strange. It suddenly occurred to her that there had been no voices. Not only voices, but no steps on the stairs, no clicking sound as Magda struggled with the tricky lock on her door. Jess sat in the dark and wondered what to do. She didn't want to get out of bed. She didn't want to open the door. She certainly didn't want to go downstairs to check the outside door. But she wouldn't get a minute's sleep unless she did.

At last, Jess reluctantly pushed aside the covers and padded across the room into her hall. At least it wasn't dark here. She'd been too jumpy to turn out the light. She unlocked the door and stepped into the dimly lit landing.

"Magda? You there?" No reply. Jess had a feeling that something wasn't right. Bad things come in threes, so they say. Two bad things had happened today and although it was gone midnight, Jess was sure the day wasn't over yet.

"Magda?" Jess heard the fear in her own voice. Gradually her eyes began to adjust to the dark in the foyer. She looked around, blinking, and her eyes made out a shape stretched out by the main door.

When Jess realised what it was, her screams reverberated around the whole house.

Magda was the first to reach her, followed by Pam and Henry. Bunty lay on the mat just inside the door, unmoving. Her chocolate brown fur was matted and her legs extended stiffly from her inert body. Jess could see froth around the dog's half-open mouth. Jess looked up at Pam, her eyes wide.

"Ees Bunty, no?" Magda's voice was a hoarse whisper. Jess nodded. Henry stepped over the dog and threw the door wide open. He looked up and down the street as if expecting to see Bunty's killer running off. Jess knew he would see no one.

Jess had her arm round Pam, whose face was buried in her shoulder. "I'm so, so sorry," Jess said.

Henry stepped back inside and tried to persuade Pam to go back upstairs, but she pushed him away. She sank to her knees beside her beloved pet. Henry made a move to stop her but Jess shook her head. Pam needed a last moment with Bunty.

"What happen to her?" Magda said.

"Looks like poison," said Henry.

Magda shook her head. "Who would do such thing to poor, dumb animal?"

They stood for a couple of minutes until Jess asked Pam if she was ready to go back to her flat.

"What about Bunty?" Pam asked. "We can't just leave her here."

"I'll get a blanket from my flat. Magda and I will cover her and put her under the stairs. I think we'd better inform the police in the morning." Jess thought of the bag of rotting organs. It was hard not to read that event as a warning of what was to follow. Eventually Pam nodded, and Henry led her, still sobbing, upstairs.

Jess and Magda stared at the dead animal. Jess sighed. "I'll fetch that blanket."

Together, she and Magda wrapped it around Bunty as best they could. The dog, already stiff with rigor, was too heavy to lift, so they ended up dragging her across the floor. Jess thanked Magda.

"What time did you get home?"

"Only one hour ago!" Magda said. "I hear door open, then a leetle while later I hear you scream."

"I thought it was you coming home from work."

"I have evening off. I go to pub with Paulo." Paulo was Magda's boyfriend. Jess looked towards Magda's door. "He not here. Early sheeft at hospital." Paulo, a qualified accountant, was working as a hospital porter. Magda yawned. "We go to bed now, yes?"

"Yes," Jess agreed, catching the yawn. Magda closed her door and Jess stood for a few moments, staring at the doormat where poor Bunty had been dumped. She had been afraid of this from the moment she heard that Bunty had disappeared. The police would assume that Pam's ex had ratcheted up his attempts to terrorise her. Jess hoped he could prove his innocence, for she was certain that Bunty's killer was someone with a far more sinister agenda. Her thoughts returned to the note. Bad things will happen to those you care about.

The following morning, Jess was woken by a loud knocking at her door. It was Pam, accompanied by Henry and the same police constable who had come in answer to their call about the bag of offal.

"I hope we didn't wake you, Jess."

Jess stood in her Minions pyjamas, rubbing sleep from her eyes.

"I called the police first thing. Didn't sleep a wink last night, thinking of how much poor Bunty must have suffered."

"I think it would have been quite quick," Henry said, and Pam glared at him. Clearly this wasn't the first time he had tried to reassure her.

"People who hurt animals hurt people too, you know," Pam said, now glaring at the police officer. Jess was reminded of Mitch's words about psychopaths. This certainly counted as an escalation.

"I can assure you, your pet's death will be properly investigated, Mrs Hollings," the officer replied. "If she was deliberately harmed, the person responsible could face a big fine or even a sentence." This seemed to upset Pam even more. Whatever the punishment, it would never be enough. Jess stood in her doorway, shivering. She excused herself and disappeared into her flat to put some clothes on. By the time she joined the others in the hallway, Pam seemed to have calmed down. Jess gave a statement to the officer.

"I'd like to take a statement from this Magda too," the PC said.

"She'll be at work. She's a carer. She often leaves at six in the morning. I'll give you her mobile number if you like." Jess turned to leave. It was time to get ready for work. As she crossed the hallway to her flat, she heard the words 'vet' and 'autopsy' and a lump rose in her throat. She hoped Henry was right and Bunty had gone quickly and without suffering.

She just had time for a shower. It was a chilly morning and steam condensed on the shower door and swirled around her in the cubicle. Being unable to see through the glass made her uneasy, and she opened the door to let it escape. After stepping out of the cubicle, she opened the small window above her washbasin and then closed it again, feeling rattled. Was this how it was going to be from now on? Feeling unsafe in her own home? How many times would she have to check the locks every day?

She wished she hadn't quarrelled with Mitch, and wondered why he hadn't been in touch. Why she hadn't been in touch with him. Her whole life was a mess. A cup of coffee and a bowl of cereal restored some perspective. Leanne was dead, the victim of a deranged and cruel killer. Pam's loss and her own boyfriend problems paled in comparison. But Jess couldn't shake the feeling that things were going to get worse.

Chapter Thirteen

"DS Merry, I'd like you to accompany me to Jeffers." Ava stared at Neal, her mouth open. Did she think he was asking her on a date? He looked at her. "The nightclub where Bryony claims to have seen Seth mistreating a girl on the pavement outside?"

"I know where you mean, sir. Sorry, I was just thinking about something Ollie said to me this morning."

Relieved, Neal asked her to meet him outside in ten minutes. Ava probably needed an injection of caffeine.

"We walking?" Ava joined him outside, blinking in the bright sunlight. The nightclub was about five minutes' walk away. It would take much longer in the car. Neal nodded and waited while she rummaged in her bag for a pair of oversized sunglasses. They added a touch of film star glamour to her already perfect looks. They walked on in silence. Neal glanced at her profile, for the first time noticing the freckles dappled across her forehead. Maybe it was the sun. He realised it had been mostly grey or dark since they began working together less than a year ago. He thought again of that moment in the car after her birthday drink, and his pulse quickened.

"So, Maggie phoned me last night," Ava said.

"Oh?" The friendship between Ava and his sister sometimes made Neal anxious that work might be coming too close to his private life.

"She seems quite smitten with your friend, Jock."

Neal smiled. "Jock's been in love with my sister for as long as I can remember." To tell the truth, he was hoping Maggie might have confided to Ava how she felt about his friend.

"Well, it looks like his love isn't going to remain unrequited for much longer."

"Did Maggie tell you she had feelings for him?" Neal looked at her.

"Hasn't she told you?"

"Not in so many words, but it's quite likely I've missed some signals." They stopped to cross the road.

"Yes, that wouldn't surprise me." Ava's face was turned towards the oncoming traffic.

"So I can tell Jock he has a chance?"

Ava looked up. "We're here."

The bar was above a pizza restaurant. After a cursory glance at their ID, the bouncer waved them up a narrow flight of stairs.

Ava smiled at Neal. "Yes, Jock has a chance."

Neal concentrated on his feet. The walls were painted matt black and it was hard to see. A man was waiting at the top.

"DI Neal? DS Merry? I'm Mackenzie Thorner, commonly known as Mac. I'm the manager. Well, owner actually. One of them. Would you like to come upstairs to my office?" They followed him across an L-shaped room that seemed surprisingly small to Neal. There was a bar, a dance floor the size of a postage stamp, a few round tables and a banquette that ran along the length of one wall. A mike and some karaoke equipment stood roughly halfway along the longer wall. Neal glanced at it, and remembered Ava's sexy performance at her birthday celebration.

Mac showed them into a small room with windows overlooking the street. He had mutton chop whiskers and a bleached white smile which was currently flashing at Ava.

She returned the smile. "Nice place you have here."

"I bought it with my brother. He's in musicals. That's him as Joseph up there, see?" He pointed to a large, framed poster above his desk. It showed a young man who looked like Mac's twin dressed in a multi-coloured coat. "He's in a show right now down in London. You might have heard of him? Lex Thorner? It's Alex really. Lex is his stage name. We always have a full house when he does a gig here. His fans come from all over." Neal thought Lex's fans must hardly be legion if they could be accommodated in a bar this size.

He smiled politely. "Mr Mackenzie, we're here in connection with an investigation into the death of a woman called Leanne Jackson."

"Terrible business," Mac said. "But how can I help?"

Neal explained that they were looking for Seth Conway.

Ava showed him the photograph forwarded by the Yeardsley Trust. "Have you seen him in the club?" Mac stared at the picture and nodded.

"How about these young women?" Ava showed Mac images of Corinna Masters and Ruby Kennedy. "No, sorry. They don't look familiar."

"Can you tell us anything about Seth Conway?" Neal asked.

"He wasn't a regular, but there was an incident involving him. A young woman picked a fight with him one night. We had to throw her out."

"Any idea what it was all about?"

Mac shook his head. "No idea. She'd never been here before, so I can't tell you who she was either."

"Does your bar have CCTV, Mac?" Ava asked.

"Yeah. My brother-in-law installed it. But we wipe the tapes after seven days. You could always try YouTube."

Neal nodded, recalling all the events he'd attended in the past few years where people filmed rather than watched the real thing. He doubted it would yield great results. The quality of amateur films shot on mobile phones was often execrable. He could never understand why people spent an entire event filming something they were there to experience live.

"It's worth a shot," Ava said.

"I could give you a list of Lex's fans that regularly tweet and put out blog posts on him, if it would help. They were all filming and blogging that night. You could check their social media sites."

"That would be great, thanks, Mac," Ava said.

They turned to leave. On their way out, Mac stamped a couple of leaflets advertising his brother's next gig at the bar. "Show these to Jake on the door and say Mac said to let you in." He rummaged in a tray on his desk. "Here, take these too." He handed them both a slip entitling them to a free drink.

"Er, sorry, we're not allowed, but thanks anyway." Neal gave Mac his contact details so that he could send on the list of bloggers. They returned, with relief, to the sunshine.

"Guess I'll be spending hours watching YouTube videos of Lex Mackenzie." Ava sounded less than enthusiastic.

"First we're going to speak with Ruby Kennedy's parents," Neal said.

Neal and Ava walked back to the station.

* * *

Within the hour they were drawing up outside a mock-Tudor style family home on an estate backing onto Silverbirch Park. This was a large country park in the southwest of the city with acres of woodland and a large lake. It had once been owned by a local businessman who had built his family home there, called Silverbirch Hall.

During the Second World War, the hall had served as an officers' mess, and the land had been used for military training. By the time the land was purchased by the city in the 1950s, the hall had fallen into disrepair. It had been demolished rather than restored, and the grounds opened to the public. In a matter of years it had an adventure playground, a visitor centre and a café.

A long strip of silver birch trees shielded the Kennedys' estate from the park's boundary walls. At this time of year the woodland fringing the park was ribboned with rhododendrons, their deep magenta blooms a striking contrast to the pale trunks of the slender birch trees.

Ava looked at her phone. "It's four thirty. We're twenty minutes early."

"They're in. I saw someone at an upstairs window," said Neal. The house was set back from the street, with similar houses on either side of it. "Come on," Neal said, impatient to get the interview over with. Ruby Kennedy's parents had already been informed of their daughter's death, but their grief would still be raw. Neal wasn't looking forward to confronting it.

The Kennedys had not seen their daughter for some time prior to her death. Ruby had a history of running away from home. Ava had contacted Ruby's social worker and heard a familiar tale of early trauma — in Ruby's case, it was a sexual assault when she was fourteen, committed by a group of boys in the park that lay just an arm's reach from her home. From being a difficult child she had spiralled into an unmanageable teenager with emotional and behavioural issues.

The woman who opened the door to them appeared to be in her late forties or early fifties. She was slight, dressed in cargo shorts and a pretty floral top. Her shoulder-length hair was streaked with blonde highlights — or lowlights, Neal was never sure which was which, though Maggie had once explained it to him. Her legs were bare, lightly tanned, and muscular. She looked as though she went to the gym two or three times a week and watched what she ate. Neal knew that she had a good job in a bank, and her husband was a maths teacher. The Kennedys had two other children besides Ruby. A surface-perfect family, with a dark and tragic underside.

Neal introduced himself and Ava, and Martha Kennedy led them through a living room furnished in oak, past a sumptuous cream soft leather sofa, into a sunlit conservatory overlooking a long, well-kept lawn. A cluster of silver birches fringed the fence at the bottom of the garden, one of them standing just inside the boundary. A wooden seat had been placed under the tree, and a man sat there, filling a bird-feeder with nuts. Martha Kennedy tapped on the conservatory window, and the man stood up and came in to join them. Douglas Kennedy was about a foot taller than his wife and at least ten years older. He looked careworn. Unlike his fashionably dressed wife, he reminded Neal of the male leads in the Bergman films of the fifties. They all had wavy hair, geeky glasses and wore oversized Scandinavian jumpers, and were invariably intellectual and introspective.

His wife introduced them. Douglas pushed his glasses further up his long nose and solemnly shook their hands. They were polite people, Neal guessed, but good manners couldn't mask the sadness that came off them in waves. No drinks were offered. They sat down in the bright conservatory — too bright, it seemed, for the dark conversation at hand.

Before Neal could begin, Martha Kennedy blurted out, "Please find who did this to our daughter. We want justice for her now, that's all." Her husband sat in stony silence, pulling at his fingers. Neal got the impression that he had learned to expect disappointment.

Before Neal could say anything, Ava, who was often given to speaking out of turn, said, "We will, Mrs Kennedy."

For once Neal didn't feel irritated with her for making such an assurance.

"Perhaps, if it's not too difficult, you could tell us something about Ruby's life," he said, gently. "Please take your time and stop if you feel distressed."

Martha waved her arms in a gesture of helplessness.

"I believe Ruby went to stay with foster parents in Nottingham because her social worker felt she was at risk here in Stromford?" Neal looked at the husband.

Douglas Kennedy sighed. "Ruby's problems started a lot longer ago than that. We should probably start further back." Beside him, his wife nodded, her eyes on the floor. "Love?" Douglas prompted.

The word seemed to galvanise Martha. Her whole demeanour went from passive, grief-stricken spouse to fierce, protective mother, someone who was more than capable of speaking for herself. This, Neal suspected, was the real Martha Kennedy. He had seen it all too often, especially with women of a certain age for whom confidence and assertiveness had been earned rather than given as a birth-right.

"We used to think we were just really bad at the business of parenting," Martha began. "Ruby was our eldest. No one knows what to expect when they have a child, but Ruby just seemed to turn everything we thought we knew on its head. She was clever, quick," Martha paused, then smiled. "Lit from within I used to say, because she seemed so full of joy and life. But she was . . . demanding. Exhausting. Even as a toddler her behaviour could be challenging. She used to hit the other kids at her play group for no apparent reason. At primary school she was disruptive in class. Douglas and I were always being called in to speak to the head teacher. Friends told us it was because she was bright, and that difficult children often grow into well-behaved, studious teenagers." Martha gave a sort of laugh. "If only. By the time she left primary school, she'd been diagnosed with ADHD—"

Douglas interrupted. "Our daughter's life might have panned out differently if it hadn't been for. . ." Douglas couldn't say it. It was left to Martha to utter the detestable word.

"The rape." Her voice was steady. She had probably talked about her daughter's experience to friends, relatives, counsellors. Unlike her husband, Neal suspected, who sat, ramrod straight on the rattan sofa, anger radiating from every cell in his body. Despite the warmth of the conservatory, Douglas Kennedy looked like he'd been dipped in liquid nitrogen.

Martha paid no attention to her husband's discomfort. "No doubt you already know about that," she said. Neal gave a slight nod. "She was walking through the park on her way home from a friend's house at about half six in the evening. It was dark. She'd been warned not to take that shortcut in the winter, but Ruby never seemed to have much sense of danger. She was thirteen at the time.

She was crossing the adventure playground when three boys from her school stopped in front of her, blocking her way. The boys were older, two of them nineteen and the other twenty. They chatted with her, gave her cigarettes and cans of cider. She thought they were just being friendly, and she enjoyed the attention. It didn't take long for her to get drunk — she'd never had alcohol before. They pushed her on the swing. Then they took turns having sex with her."

PJ had spoken with Ruby's social worker, who had told her that Ruby hadn't really understood the gravity of what had happened to her. She had identified the boys after her distraught parents alerted the police, but had been unable to grasp that they had done anything all that wrong. Though charges had been brought against the boys, they had been dropped because Ruby would not speak out against them.

"That's when our lives began to unravel," Martha said, her voice trembling now. "Ruby's behaviour spiralled out of control. She was hardly ever at school. One evening a girl from her class turned up on our doorstep and asked if we knew Ruby was sneaking out late at night and hanging round with a group of older boys. We didn't really believe this tale until Doug waited outside the house one night and saw her climb out of her bedroom window onto the roof of the porch, and jump to the ground. He followed her to the park where he saw her flirting with some boys and knocking back booze. He waited until she climbed into the back seat of a car with two of the lads before he intervened. He dragged her kicking and screaming from the car and as soon as he got her home, she tried to go out again. We had to physically restrain her from leaving the house." Martha choked up and turned aside.

"Would you like to take a break?" Neal asked. "I appreciate this must be very traumatic for you."

"If you point me in the direction of the kitchen, I could make some tea — or coffee," Ava offered. Martha nodded.

"Please excuse me for a few minutes," Martha said. "I'll be right back."

"I'll show you where everything is." Douglas stood up and Ava followed him out. Neal went to the window and watched a squirrel trying to steal nuts from the bird-feeder. He stepped outside for some fresh air, startling the squirrel.

At times like these, Neal felt like a voyeur, an intruder in the lives of grieving families. He had to do it, of course, it was part of the job, but he would never get used to it. Was it really that crucial to the case to hear these distraught parents recount their story? He had learned no new facts.

Voices wafted through the open kitchen window. He heard the throaty sound of Ava's infectious laughter. Well, Douglas Kennedy had enough darkness in his life. Let him bask in Ava's light for a while. The sound of running water indicated that Martha was washing away her tears. He marvelled at the couple's ability to carry on in the face of such tragedy. The Kennedys' marriage must have been tested to breaking point by worry over their daughter. Had they ever wished her out of their lives for good? They didn't strike him as the sort of people who would abandon their responsibilities, or renounce their unconditional love when things got tough.

Martha retuned first. She joined Neal in the garden and he told her about the squirrel.

Martha smiled. "The nuts are for him too, but he's greedy. We leave titbits for him on the bird table but he eats them and then wants the birds' food too."

From the kitchen came the sound of Ava's laughter again. This time, Neal could hear Douglas joining in.

Martha said quietly, "I'm grateful to your sergeant. I don't often hear Doug laughing these days." She looked at Neal. "Do you have children?"

"One. A son. He's ten, nearly eleven," Neal replied, embarrassed at the pride in his voice.

"We have twin boys as well as Ruby. It hasn't been easy for them, especially when they were younger and Ruby was kicking off all the time. She could be quite aggressive at times, but never towards them. They adored her."

Neal found himself echoing Ava's assurance. "We will get justice for you and Ruby, Mrs Kennedy."

Ava waved at them from the conservatory. Douglas was behind her, carrying a tea tray. "Shall we go back in?" Martha led the way.

Once inside, Douglas passed Neal a milk jug. "DS Merry has been telling me about her prowess in the martial arts. Used to do a bit of karate and judo myself. I taught Ruby and the boys a few moves. I'm afraid I'm no match for your sergeant though."

Neal smiled. "Tell me how Ruby ended up in care." He felt like the greedy squirrel, wanting more than its due.

Martha sighed. "Ruby became known to social services at the time of the rape. We'd hoped they'd be some real help to her, but that was a laugh. Do you have any idea of the shambolic state of mental health services available to vulnerable young people?"

Child and adolescent mental health services — CAMHS — were in a state of crisis. There were abundant stories in the news about teenage suicides that occurred because young people had to wait too long for professional help, but that was only the tip of the iceberg. A whole generation of young people with many different kinds of mental health issues was being denied access to any kind of care.

"Even if you are lucky enough to see someone, nine times out of ten they just want to dope your kid to make them compliant. The drugs they tried giving Ruby just seemed to make her worse and she refused to take them. As for social workers, you have to have a thick skin when you're dealing with them. Like teachers, they lay the blame for a child's behaviour on the parents. I tried asking them why I had two perfectly behaved sons who were brought up in exactly the same way, and no one could give me an answer. Didn't fit with their preconceived ideas."

Martha was shaking with anger by now. Douglas took hold of his wife's hand. "Calm down, love."

"I'm sorry."

"No need to apologise," Neal said.

"I'm sorry because I haven't answered your question yet. Things went from bad to worse. We struggled to keep Ruby indoors. Sometimes it felt like we were imprisoning her, Inspector. Whatever we did, she always managed to sneak out somehow and put herself in danger. There were fights, screaming matches, the twins began to suffer. I ended up on anti-depressants and Doug was in danger of losing his job because he had to take so much time off work — by that time I was already on long term sick leave. Finally, we had to sign Ruby over to social services and they put her into foster care. It was a terrible time for all of us, not least Ruby, who couldn't understand why we were doing it."

"It didn't end there, though," Douglas said. "Almost immediately, Ruby started disappearing from her foster home. We tried to have her transferred to some kind of facility where she would have adult supervision — a home basically, where she'd have minders with her all the time and where she could get the right sort of help."

"Then she turned eighteen and, of course, adult mental health services are as chaotic as those for children and young people . . ." Martha's voice trailed off.

"We lost her, Officers. Our daughter disappeared from our lives. By the time we received the news of her death, we had no idea where she was." The light had gone out of Douglas Kennedy again. He sat there, a man in ruins.

Ava took a brown envelope from her bag. It contained photographs of Leanne Jackson and the names of the women on her list.

Douglas Kennedy looked at the envelope. "Have you come to talk to us about something else besides our daughter, Detectives?"

"We wanted to ask you about the other young woman who died on the same night as Ruby. You might have heard her death reported on the local news? Her name was Leanne Jackson. What we'd like to know is whether your daughter knew Leanne."

Ava pulled Leanne's photograph from the envelope and placed it on the table. Martha Kennedy gave it a quick glance, then said, "I spoke with her on the phone a couple of weeks ago." Her husband looked at her, puzzled.

Neal and Ava exchanged looks. "Why did Leanne contact you?" Ava asked.

"She said she knew Ruby from years ago." Martha gave a sniff and Douglas passed her his handkerchief. "She didn't say where from. Maybe school, I don't know. We heard about Leanne on the news, of course. Then the news about Ruby came and everything else went out of my head."

Douglas Kennedy shook his head. "I don't recall Ruby ever mentioning someone called Leanne."

"Is it possible that your daughter returned to Stromford when she came out of foster care?" Ava said. Neal had opened his mouth to ask the same question.

The Kennedys exchanged glances. Douglas sounded irate. "Of course it is. When we lost touch with Ruby, we asked the Nottinghamshire police to alert the police in the Stromfordshire area."

Ava glanced at Neal and he shook his head. "We'll look into that, Mr Kennedy. We're used to cooperating with other forces but if the information wasn't communicated to us . . ." Neal realised he sounded as if he were making excuses. The Kennedys deserved better than that.

Neal gave Ava a nod and she took the other photographs from the envelope and laid them out around Leanne's.

"How about these young women? Are any of them familiar?" Ava asked. Martha pointed to the picture of a young woman with a very distinguishing feature — one eye was blue, the other brown.

"Alyssa," Martha said, wonderingly. "She was in Ruby's year at school. Why are you showing us these pictures, DI Neal?" Her hand went to her throat. "Something's happened to all of them, hasn't it? Are they all. .?"

"Alyssa is alive and well. She emigrated to Australia five years ago." Ava pointed to the picture of Chantelle Clarke. "Chantelle Clarke. She took her own life. Michaela Howard died trying to rescue a dog."

"But you think there might be something more to their deaths, don't you?" Douglas said. Neal decided to level with him.

"Truthfully? We don't know, but yes, we do have some concerns."

Ava looked at him, and Neal gave a nod.

"We don't have a photo, but there's one other woman we'd like to ask you about. Her name is Corinna Masters." The Kennedys shook their heads. Martha's eyes were glistening with tears again, but Ava pressed on.

When it comes to police work, she is all steel, Neal thought.

"Given that Ruby's body was found near Stromford, it's possible that she came back here, and was living somewhere in or near the city. Who would she go to?" Ava asked.

Neal closed his eyes momentarily. She might as well have kicked the Kennedys in the stomach.

"Not to us, obviously, Sergeant," Douglas said icily.

The atmosphere had changed. Neal looked at his watch. "Thank you for your cooperation, Mr and Mrs Kennedy. Once more, I'm truly sorry for your loss."

"Just one more question," Ava said, with an apologetic glance at Neal. "You told us that Ruby received medication for a bit when her behaviour went off the rails. I know you said that you hoped social services would help Ruby. Did she attend any group counselling sessions at CAMHS as part of her treatment?"

"Yes, to both questions," Martha replied.

"Thank you," Ava said quietly. The Kennedys saw them to the door.

As soon as they were out of earshot, Ava said, "I'll check the dates when Ruby attended CAMHS." Neal nodded. He had little doubt about what she would discover.

* * *

The house was quiet when Neal returned from work that evening. Archie had gone to a friend's birthday party and Maggie was busy in the kitchen cooking up something special, which seemed suspicious to Neal, as it wasn't even her cooking night. If she were trying to impress Jock, she was going the wrong way about it. Maggie was a competent cook, nothing more. Normally she stuck with what she was good at, but judging by the unfamiliar smells wafting from the kitchen every time she opened the door, this was going to be one of her 'experimental' meals. He hoped she'd keep it simple. He found Jock in the lounge reading one of his true crime books, glass of scotch in hand.

Jock laid the book aside. "Smells braw whatever she's cookin."

"Aye, well, don't expect too much," Neal cautioned.

"Ach, Jim, that woman could serve me a battered Mars bar and I'd eat it with a smile on my face. So how's the case going?"

Neal wasn't in the habit of discussing the cases he was working on but he made an exception for his friend. Jock, a doctor, was used to respecting confidentiality. He whistled softly when Neal told him.

"A suicide and a drowning that could be related to two murders. How are you keeping this out of the papers, Jim?"

"Partly because we've only just started joining up the dots ourselves. No one's linked these women before."

"The lassie who drowned, Michaela, was it? Had she been drinking?"

"Tox report showed a fair amount of alcohol in her bloodstream. She was also on Ritalin for her ADHD."

"Which would interact with the alcohol in her bloodstream. Ritalin's a stimulant and alcohol's a depressant, but that doesn't mean they cancel each other out. She may not have realised how drunk she was, poor lass. I'd expect the dog to have survived. Do you know what breed it was?"

Neal shrugged. "Labrador retriever, I think."

"They're good swimmers. If it was healthy, there's no reason why it should perish. Maybe the witness got it the wrong way around and the dog went into the water to rescue the girl. Could have tired itself out trying to rescue her and couldn't make it back to the riverbank."

Neal looked sceptical.

"I wonder what became of the poor pooch." Jock was a dog lover. He had a dog called Lachie who often accompanied Neal and Jock on their hillwalking expeditions. "I know that in instances of suspected animal cruelty a forensic necropsy can take place. .."

"A local vet disposed of the body. As far as I know it was incinerated." He looked at Jock. "Damn, you're right. It might have been relevant. The dog could have been drugged or poisoned, or even chucked in the water already dead. I doubt anyone bothered to check."

Both men were silent. The blaring of the smoke alarm startled them. Neal rushed to the door and was assaulted by the smell of burning.

Maggie, looking harassed, was waving a tea towel at the ceiling. "Nothing's burning. These things are so bloody sensitive. I should have taken the batteries out before I started with the frying pan.

"Something's definitely burning." Neal sniffed the air, earning a glare from his sister.

Maggie ushered him out. "Everything's under control. I'll call you when it's ready. Shouldn't be too long."

Back in the living room, Neal grumbled, "I hate it when she starts trying to do fancy stuff. Usually ends in beans on toast."

"It didn't smell that bad to me. You're fussing over nothing," Jock said.

Neal rolled his eyes. He doubted whether Jock would notice anything Maggie served him up. He would need to be careful what he said to Jock about his sister from now on. He sighed. The case was demanding enough without having to deal with a love-struck Jock. Affairs of the heart were not really his forte.

"Well, I'm here for a couple of weeks, Jim. Let me know if I can help you out in any way. I might as well make myself useful. I could play Dr Watson to your Sherlock Holmes. What d'ye think of that as an idea?

"Er . . ." To Neal's relief, Maggie popped her head around the door to announce that dinner was ready.

Chapter Fourteen

Following the macabre discovery of Bunty's body, Jess had developed a habit of looking over her shoulder. She felt vulnerable, but more than that, she couldn't shake the feeling that people close to her might be in danger because of something she'd done. But what was it? Why? The threatening note had advised her to stop looking into things that didn't concern her if she didn't want people close to her to get hurt. If it hadn't been for the recent incidents she might have dismissed it as a prank. On balance, she still thought Michael must be responsible. She couldn't think of anyone else. Jess baulked at the thought of bringing this up with Pam. Her friend had been through a lot in the past few days and Jess had no wish to upset her further.

In her morning break, Jess popped out to go to the bank. Hurrying across the campus, she looked upon familiar and unfamiliar faces alike with suspicion. Even standing in the queue at the bank, she felt anxious.

Back at college, in the busy corridor outside the classrooms, she felt safer.

"Jess! Hi!"

It was Jonty Cole. She hadn't seen him since the day they'd had coffee together. She hadn't seen Mitch either. Jonty seemed self-conscious.

"I just wanted to apologise for the other day," he began.

"What for? We're friends, aren't we?" Jess said.

Jonty peered at her. "Are you alright, Jess? You look kind of tired."

"I'm fine. Just didn't get a lot of sleep last night."

"Big night out, was it?"

"Oh no, nothing like that. Just . . . just a bit of trouble at my place."

"Oh? What kind of trouble? If you don't mind me asking."

"I . . . it's a bit of a long story." He was beginning to irritate her again.

"Well, if you need someone to talk to . . ."

"Thanks, Jonty. That's kind of you, but I'm fine."

"What about after work? I could pick you up."

Really? "I, er, actually I'm seeing my boyfriend later."

He nodded. "Ah, yes. Mitch, isn't it? Well, he's a lucky guy, Jess. I hope he appreciates you."

Jess smiled politely. Jonty stepped a little closer to her. Too close. For a moment, she thought he was going to kiss her. She flinched, and instinctively took a step backwards.

"S . . . sorry, Jess."

Jess looked up and down the corridor, glad to see that there were other people about, though she still felt vulnerable.

"Er . . . excuse me, Jonty. I need to get to my classroom now." Jess moved to the side so that she could get past him, but Jonty still hovered. Jess wished he'd just get the message and go away. She had a feeling there was something more he wanted to say. But after a moment or two, all he said was, "Sorry for holding you up. Have a nice day, Jess."

Why had he started with all that again after she'd made it clear in the coffee shop that even if she weren't already dating, she still wouldn't be interested? Was he just a nice, persistent guy who was a bit dumb? Or was he a creep who used his disabled brother to ingratiate himself with women?

Why had he been here anyway? She looked around for Barney. He was standing with a group of friends further down the corridor. Had Jonty even spoken to him? Jess spotted a colleague and asked her if Jonty had been to see Barney. The answer was reassuring. He had brought Barney's swimming trunks, which he'd forgotten to pack that morning. A perfectly sound explanation. Unless . . . unless Jonty had deliberately not packed them as a pretext for coming to college. To see her. So what? If he did fancy her, he'd be looking for ways to engineer meetings with her. She had to stop being so paranoid.

Still anxious, Jess decided that it might be a good move to talk to Ava Merry about the recent events. She called Ava's number after work and was relieved to hear the detective's friendly voice.

"I was just wondering," Jess began, "if you're going to be at the pool tomorrow morning?"

"Yes, would you like to talk again?" Ava asked. "I'm afraid I don't have much news for you."

"That's okay. I just wanted to ask you something, that's all."

Ava must have picked up on her anxiety, for she said, "Are you alright, Jess? Has something happened? Is it something to do with Leanne?"

"Some bad things have happened over the past couple of days. I'd just like to run them past you to see what you think. It's probably nothing, I expect I'm just overreacting . . ."

"Would you like to see me sooner, Jess? I could meet you this evening if you like."

Jess considered Ava's offer. Supposing Mitch came round to make up? "Tomorrow morning will do. Like I said, it's probably just me being paranoid."

They agreed to meet in the pool café after their swim.

On her way home, Jess called into Marks and Spencer to buy some flowers for Pam. She planned to call round later that evening to see how she was coping. Just in case Mitch did turn up, she also bought a nice bottle of wine.

She walked home along the river, stopping for a few moments at the place where she had seen the police divers searching the Strom for clues.

The riverside path was surprisingly quiet. It was nice to be able to enjoy these quiet times of day, but Jess was conscious, as always, that these were hours when she could be working. She'd all but decided by now that she had to find some way of earning more money, even if it meant running up a huge debt to do a degree.

In her teens she had lacked confidence because of her scoliosis, but she had gained a lot of self-esteem from working and from friends like Pam. Working as a support assistant was rewarding personally, but like most jobs that involved caring for people, it was poorly paid. Her neighbour, Magda, worked ridiculously long hours providing personal care, mostly to elderly people. She took on extra hours whenever she could and was dedicated to her clients, yet some months she struggled to live within her budget. The private company she worked for paid her a fraction of what it charged to provide care. Magda did it because she could send money home to her mother and her six-year-old son, and because it was far more than she could earn in Poland. People were all that mattered, Jess thought, so why did caring for them seem to matter so little?

Mitch had said he didn't mind what Jess did or how much she earned, but she was conscious of the fact that if they stayed together they might one day want to save for a mortgage. *If* they stayed together. With a pang of regret,

Jess realised she didn't want to lose him. She didn't really think he was possessive or controlling. She'd overreacted. Pam, ever the cynic since her recent break-up, had told her what the warning signs were, and now she was over cautious. If she heard that Mitch had been drinking coffee with another woman, perhaps the green-eyed monster would get hold of her too. Reversing the male and female roles sometimes helped put things in perspective.

This silly row over Jonty had shown her a side of Mitch that was troubling, but there was something else. At some subconscious level she still believed she was not worthy of his love. Love? The word took her by surprise and she shelved it quickly.

Jess approached her flat and her pace slowed. A feeling of trepidation accompanied her to the entrance door. She fumbled in her handbag and pulled out a shiny new key — the letting agency had been sympathetic after what happened to Bunty and had changed the locks at last.

She stepped into the hallway, unable to stop herself picturing Bunty lying there on her side, her velvety mouth gaping, her tongue lolling out in a pool of frothy saliva. With a shudder, she closed the door and turned to face the wide staircase leading up to Pam's flat. Should she go straight up to Pam's? After a moment's indecision, she ran up the stairs, only to find a note on Pam's door to say that she'd gone to the cinema.

Disappointed, Jess made her way back downstairs. At this time of day, Magda would be at work so there was no point on knocking on her door either. Edgy, she stepped into the hallway of her own flat.

"Pull yourself together, Jessica Stoke," she said aloud. She had to overcome this uneasiness about being home alone. Funny, with Pam above her and Magda down the hallway, she hadn't felt that she did live alone until now. It struck her that at this moment she was not just alone in her flat, but was the only person in the whole building.

Jess tossed her handbag onto the floor, hung up her jacket and kicked off her ankle boots. She made for her bedroom, changed into a pair of boyfriend jeans and an oversized T shirt, and slipped on a pair of flip flops.

"Right. Let's put the kettle on." She spoke aloud to break the silence. In the kitchen, she turned on the radio for company.

The kitchen was at the back of the flat. It had a window looking out towards the garden, which was obscured from view by the brick wall of an unused garage just outside. Someone had tried to compensate for the view by painting the wall with a cheerful mural of a garden, complete with gnomes. Sometimes it worked for her, sometimes it didn't. Today, it didn't. She longed for a glimpse of a long, sunlit lawn, not gloomy brickwork dotted with dark green moss and half in shadow. She gave a sudden shiver and felt goose bumps tingle along the length of her bare arms. She caught sight of what seemed an uncharacteristically malevolent grin on the face of the nearest gnome. He'd never looked this creepy before.

It was a small kitchen, with not much room to swing the proverbial cat, but it had a large, airy, old-fashioned pantry, and Jess could feel a draught through the half-open door leading two steps down to where she kept her fridge and the milk she needed for her coffee. She froze.

It wasn't the draught that bothered her.

It was the fact that the door was weighted to self-close and it was standing open.

A shadow moved, just visible through the gap between the door and the lintel.

"Mitch?" she said, hesitantly. No reply. "This isn't funny, Mitch. You're scaring me."

The door jerked open. Someone who was not Mitch crossed to her in a single stride. Jess screamed, the man lunged, then everything went dark.

* * *

Pam Hollis was worried. She had been expecting Jess to pop up to see her the day after they'd found poor Bunty's body in the hallway. Jess had messaged her first thing in the morning to ask how she was and how she was coping, saying that she'd call round after work. The kettle had been turned on in anticipation, but Pam had ended up drinking her coffee alone. Eventually she sat down with her laptop and tried to work, but she couldn't concentrate. She kept thinking of Bunty, and now Jess too.

Six o'clock came and went, and Jess still hadn't turned up. Perhaps she had gone shopping, or was otherwise occupied. It wasn't like her to be thoughtless, though. Magda had popped in between shifts and brought Pam a pretty bunch of flowers. Around ten, Pam nipped downstairs and knocked on Jess's door. No answer. There was no light shining under the door. Nothing particularly odd about that, Jess could be having an early night. Maybe it was because of Bunty, but Pam couldn't shake a feeling of unease.

In the morning she messaged Jess and received no answer. Okay. Understandable. No need for panic. If she were at work, Jess wouldn't be able to reply immediately. But when another afternoon and evening went by without her hearing from her friend, Pam really began to panic. She checked with Magda. Magda hadn't seen Jess either, but then again, she had worked fifteen out of the last twenty-four hours. She'd seen no one but her clients and her bed.

Pam also messaged Henry, but he hadn't replied either. He didn't check his mobile regularly, she knew, but it seemed odd that he hadn't been in touch since Bunty's death. She thought of going for a walk on the west common to see if he were out walking Boris, but couldn't face it without Bunty. And besides, she didn't want to seem desperate. She'd only known Henry for a few days and though he'd seemed interested, maybe the Bunty thing had scared him off.

That night, Pam went to bed disappointed and increasingly worried about Jess's failure to get in touch. She turned out her light, thinking she would contact that policewoman Jess had told her about. What was her name? Ah yes. Ava. Ava Merry.

She called early in the morning. PJ put the call through, rather confused. "It's some woman claiming her neighbour knows you from the swimming pool."

Ava frowned. After her no show at the pool the previous morning, she'd been meaning to contact Jess to ask if she were alright. As soon as she picked up the phone the breathless caller bombarded her with a flood of bizarre and seemingly random words. Ava heard 'dead dog' and 'bag of organs' and 'mugging' and 'punctured tyres,' all repeated several times.

"Slow down, Mrs . . .?"

"Hollings. Pam Hollings. I live in the same block as Jess. I haven't seen her for the best part of two days and it's not like her to go off without telling me."

"Wait a minute." Ava was beginning to grasp why this Pam was contacting her. "Are you telling me you think Jess is missing?" She thought of Jess's broken appointment with her at the pool.

"Yes. She wouldn't just disappear without telling me. Especially not after what happened to poor Bunty."

Ava heard her sniffling. "Bunty?"

"Yes. She was murdered two days ago. You know about it. A police officer came round and took all the details. They came and picked up her body so that the vet could do an autopsy."

"The vet?"

"Look, would it be better if I came down to the station? I'm really concerned about Jess and we don't seem to be getting anywhere on the phone."

The call was on speaker. PJ, listening in, stuck a finger to her temple. The woman must be crazy.

Ava turned away. "She was supposed to meet me yesterday morning at the swimming pool. She didn't show up." Pam Hollings's silence was telling. "How soon can you get here?" Ava asked. "I've got an appointment at eleven but I could fit you in for half an hour if you can come more or less immediately."

"I'll be with you in ten minutes."

Pam Hollings was a minute early. She arrived, breathless and dishevelled, as though she had thrown on some clothes and run all the way to the station. Ava showed her into a small interview room, signalling for PJ to follow. Pam declined PJ's offer of a drink.

They sat down, with Ava facing her. "So, you last saw Jess, when?"

"The night before last. It was Jess who found Bunty. On the floor in the entrance hall to our flats. We heard her screaming and came running down the stairs — except Magda of course — she lives on the ground floor, same as Jess. Jess knows what Bunty means to me. She promised to call round after work but she didn't turn up. I heard nothing from her all day yesterday. It's completely out of character for her to let a friend down. She's a lovely girl, Jess."

"And you say that you reported the incident to the police?" PJ had already pulled up the attending officer's report. He had logged Bunty's death and her body had indeed been referred for animal autopsy.

"Yes. It was the same man who came out the night Jess and Magda found the bag of offal. PC Slade." Ava nodded. She knew him by sight. PJ had also found PC Slade's report on the previous incident. He had sent the bag of offal to forensics and it had been confirmed to be animal in origin, probably pig. A nasty prank, he had concluded, but he had noted that a collar belonging to Pam Hollings's dog had been found in the bag. He had made a note that Pam's ex-husband might have been responsible and was intending to pay him a visit. It never happened. PJ pointed out that PC Slade had gone off on long term sick leave after injuring his back.

Ava was inclined to agree with Slade about the ex-husband, but Jess's disappearance was worrying. Was it just coincidence that she had a past connection with one of their victims? It was certainly worth following up, particularly if Jess didn't turn up in the next twenty-four hours.

In the meantime, Ava sought to reassure Pam. "We'll contact Jess's family and her workplace to see if she's advised them of her whereabouts. In the meantime, try not to worry. I'm sure nothing sinister has happened to Jess."

Pam sighed. "I am really worried. You know that young woman who drowned in the Strom last week?"

"Leanne Jackson?"

"Jess knew her. She was very upset about it."

"Yes. I know Jess a little. She spoke with me about it at the swimming pool last week. I wasn't able to tell her much as it's an ongoing investigation and I can't discuss details of the case. I hoped I'd managed to set her mind at rest."

Pam shook her head. "She told me she was going to try to find out what happened to Leanne herself. I told her to leave it to the police, but I don't think she was listening. Did she tell you about how Leanne helped her when she was bullied at school? About the times later on when she pretended not to know her?" Ava nodded. "I think she feels terribly guilty about that. Guilt is a strong motivator, Sergeant."

Ava was beginning to appreciate Pam's anxiety. "Did Jess speak with you about this again? About whether she'd found anything out?"

"No. We were all preoccupied over Bunty's disappearance and then her death and, like I said, I haven't seen Jess since it happened."

"Okay. I can understand your concern, Mrs Hollings. Jess works at the FE College, doesn't she? I'll give them a ring today and see if she's turned up for work or taken some leave. And as I said, we'll check with her family as well."

Pam nodded, looking relieved.

"I'm so sorry about your dog," Ava said. "I've got a cat. He, I mean, she — I've only just found out Camden's a girl — means a lot to me. I'd be heartbroken if anything happened to her."

Pam smiled for the first time. "Bless you."

After she had gone, Ava tracked down the officer who was following up on PC Slade's workload.

"Funnily enough," the PC said, "I've just been in touch with the vet and she's confirmed that the poor dog was poisoned. Anti-freeze, she thinks. Most likely forced down its throat. Who would do that to a poor animal?"

Plenty of people, Ava thought grimly. The PC must be new to the job and a bit unworldly. She'd need to toughen up.

"Have you been in touch with Pam Hollings's ex-husband?" Ava asked. "PC Slade's initial report mentioned that he should be questioned as a likely suspect." Silence.

"And?"

"Not yet. Would you like me to do that today?"

Ava counted to three in her head before producing one of her sweetest smiles. Wasted, of course, on the phone.

"That might be a good idea. Please let me know the result."

Chapter Fifteen

PJ was surprised at how readily Michaela Howard's mother agreed to a visit. Tom wasn't answering his phone, so she left him a message and drove to the estate northeast of the city where Michaela's mother lived. Patsy Howard was looking out of her kitchen window when PJ drew up, and by the by the time PJ got out of her car, she was waiting in her doorway, arms folded defensively rather than belligerently across her chest. PJ got an impression of someone emotionally frail and damaged.

"I'm so sorry to have to be speaking to you about your daughter's death, Mrs Howard," PJ began. "I know the last thing you need is to be reminded of the tragedy."

Patsy Howard waved a hand. "It must be important or you wouldn't be here, Detective. You said it was in connection with a current investigation?"

"Yeees," PJ was more truthful now that she had a foot in the door. "I'm helping with the investigation into Leanne Jackson's murder."

"I read about that in the Courier. So sad. Of course it made me think of Michaela because of her being found in the river, but she didn't drown, did she? It wasn't really like

Michaela. My daughter was a heroine. She gave her life trying to save that dog. It was a Labrador, I think. A retriever. Golden. Michaela loved animals." She gave a shrill laugh. Her thoughts were all over the place, her words just trying to fit them, or so it seemed to PJ. Still, it didn't take her long to catch on to the real reason for PJ's visit.

"Why are you asking about Leanne? Are you saying that my daughter might have been murdered too, Detective?"

PJ sighed. The last thing she wanted to do was cause Patsy Howard more distress.

"That's not why I'm here, Mrs Howard. I'm just sort of . . . gathering information." To PJ's relief (and surprise) Patsy seemed to relax. Medication, PJ thought, something to keep her emotions in check. "Er, I've been researching a link between Leanne Jackson and another case that we're investigating — that of Chantelle Clarke?"

Patsy frowned. "Chantelle Clarke? The name sounds familiar. Maybe Michaela knew her at school. No, wait a minute, I think she was probably in a therapy group my daughter attended at CAMHS."

Hadn't Ruby Kennedy's mother said something about group therapy? But it had been a different sort of therapy. Anger management? Someone was supposed to be following up on that. It had to do with Leanne's boyfriend at the time. Was this a possible connection between the women on Leanne's list? Had they all attended some sort of therapy group?

"We were told our daughter might have had something called 'borderline personality disorder.' It was a tentative diagnosis. They couldn't seem to agree on what was wrong with her. She also suffered from depression, but only because it took so bloody long for us to get a diagnosis. A lot of people don't believe mental health disorders like ADHD or autistic spectrum disorder are real illnesses. They think it's just bad parenting. Huh. An earlier diagnosis might have helped us get support for Michaela. It might have helped her to understand her condition and deal with it better. Instead she ended up being socially isolated and feeling she was worthless. No wonder she got depressed." She glared at PJ as though she, as part of the establishment, was somehow complicit in the treatment Michaela had received. Then she attempted a smile. "Sorry. I tend to get on my soapbox about the subject."

"I'm sorry too," PJ said. "It's shameful that kids like Michaela are so badly served by the system."

"Eventually Michaela started attending a group therapy session. Once a week at the CAMHS centre on Hope Street — apt location for a service like that, don't you think?" Patsy gave an ironic laugh. "I wasn't encouraged to attend with her. They said young people often feel freer to talk if their parents aren't around. Understandable, I suppose. I used to drive Michaela there and go for a coffee while I waited for her to finish."

"Did you ever meet any of the other members of the group when you dropped her off or picked her up?"

"Not really. There was nowhere to park outside the building so I'd drop her and park at the Tesco's round the corner. Michaela phoned me when she finished and we'd meet at the car."

"Did she talk much about the group, or the other kids who attended?"

"Not much." Patsy began picking at her fingers. Her emotions were raw, even though it had been a year since her daughter drowned. PJ felt bad at having to bring it all up again. Particularly as she suspected Patsy's own mental health was now in a brittle state. Ava was so much better at this, she could stick her heart up her sleeve when she needed to. PJ just wanted to give Patsy a hug.

"Excuse me a moment." Patsy left the room, and PJ heard the sound of a tap running in the kitchen, the clink of a glass, and one of those childproof caps being twisted off a bottle of pills.

While she was out of the room, PJ had a look around. Her gaze was drawn to the windowsill where an array of family photographs partially blocked the view of the street outside. The Howards had two other children besides Michaela, a boy who looked older and a girl quite a bit younger. One picture in particular made her heart ache for Patsy. It showed a more recent Howard family photograph, minus Michaela. PJ wanted children as soon as possible, but her partner, Steve, thought they should wait, have a few nice holidays and save for a mortgage first. We'll have at least three, PJ decided. Just in case.

Patsy returned and caught her looking. "I remembered something," she said. "It's probably not worth mentioning, but . . ." PJ waited. "Michaela had a crush on her therapist, well, not her therapist exactly. He was a trainee mental health nurse, I think. He sat in on some of her sessions. Observing, I suppose. She never stopped going on about him. I didn't bother about it at first. Young girls have crushes, don't they? But she got so obsessive about him that I got in touch with CAMHS behind her back and asked if she could be transferred to a different group. Not that I thought there was anything . . . you know . . . not that I thought he was doing anything to encourage her . . ." PJ sensed a 'but' coming. "But she did have a picture of him on her mobile phone . . . and I think she was sending him messages."

"What happened when you contacted CAMHS?"

"They told me he'd finished his placement there and that it was unlikely Michaela would see him again as he was doing a placement in Nottinghamshire next."

"Can you remember his name?" PJ asked.

"Seth something? Connors? No, wait, I think it was Conway. Yeah, that's it."

"Oh!" PJ bent and fiddled with her pen to hide her surprise.

Patsy's mood suddenly changed again. "Something's not right. Why are you asking me all these questions? I thought you were investigating this Leanne Jackson's murder. What do Michaela and this other woman you mentioned, Chantelle Clarke, have to do with Leanne Jackson?"

"I, er . . . It's just something we're pursuing as part of the investigation." PJ hated being evasive.

"It's more than that, though, isn't it? You think something else is going on. My God, you think someone killed all three of these young women, my Michaela included, don't you? But Michaela drowned. I don't understand."

"No, no, that's not the case at all." Patsy was teetering on the verge of hysteria, and PJ felt way out of her depth. "Mrs Howard, please don't jump to conclusions. Look, I promise I'll let you know if we have the slightest reason to believe that your daughter's death was not an accident." Shit, what a mess. PJ felt she was digging herself in deeper with every word. "Please don't talk to anyone about this, Mrs Howard. It might jeopardise our whole investigation." To PJ's relief, Patsy seemed to be calming down. For a few moments neither of them spoke.

"I'd better go now. Are you going to be alright?" PJ asked.

"What? Yes." Her mood had altered again, the pills were evidently kicking in.

Patsy saw her to the door. Her manner was distant now. "Goodbye, Sergeant. Thank you for coming." Before PJ could respond, Patsy had shut the door.

* * *

Ava intercepted PJ as soon as she walked into the station, and pulled her into the kitchen. "The DI's had a call from Michaela Howard's mother. She was practically hysterical, apparently. He couldn't understand what she was on about at first, but it seems that she's got it into her head that we're investigating a triple murder, including Michaela's."

PJ sat down. "Oh, crap."

"It gets worse. She's asking why the public hasn't been informed there's a serial killer on the loose."

PJ put her head in her hands. "Shit, shit, shit."

"What the hell did you say to her, Peej?"

PJ recounted her conversation with Patsy Howard. When she got to the part about Seth Conway, Ava whistled.

"Well, that piece of information might just be enough to stop him firing you on the spot. You'll still get a bollocking, mind." PJ nodded miserably. Ava crossed to the fridge, took out a jug and poured her friend some iced tea. "It's not all doom and gloom," she said. "Tom's been in touch with Chantelle Clarke's parents."

"I suppose he didn't cock up his interview," PJ said dismally.

Ava ignored her self-pity. "It was a different sort of interview," she said, tactfully. "It turns out that Chantelle's parents never bought the suicide thing. Chantelle had an eating disorder. She was eventually diagnosed with an autistic spectrum disorder. Apparently a lot of girls with anorexia actually have an ASD. Anyway, once Chantelle was diagnosed correctly she made good progress. She was well informed about her condition and very positive about it. Apparently at the time of her suicide, she'd been coming off her pills for depression. Her mother said that Chantelle was at," Ava made air quotation marks, "'a very positive stage in her life.' Better than she'd been for years."

"Wow."

"That's right. The Clarkes told the police all this at the time, but they feel their concerns were ignored. But get this, Peej. Chantelle didn't take the pills at home. She was found in the park — with a half-empty bottle of water and an empty packet of pills."

PJ gave a low whistle. "Someone could have forced her to take them."

Ava nodded.

"Where are we on tracing Seth Conway?" PJ asked.

"We're nowhere," Ava said. "He simply disappeared after leaving the Yeardsley Trust."

"It can't be coincidence that he knew both Leanne and Michaela. And Chantelle attended CAMHS too."

"And Ruby Kennedy. I checked the dates when she attended counselling there and they fit," Ava said. "Your discovery this morning adds to the picture. I'd say Seth Conway is our man most wanted at the moment."

DI Neal agreed. He'd appeared out of nowhere, but had obviously overheard at least some of their conversation.

"Sir . . ." PJ began.

Neal ignored her. "Ava. Get in touch with CAMHS and find out as much as you can about Seth Conway's time there. See if you can arrange to speak to someone straight away." Only then did Neal turn to PJ. "DS Jenkins. My office. Now."

Ava found Tom Knight poring over the case files. He made the call to CAHMS and was advised that the psychologist who could help them most wasn't going to be available for a few days.

"The receptionist said that a woman called Philippa Patterson might be able to help us. She was Seth Conway's mentor on his mental health nursing course. She's based at the county." He made another call and turned to Ava. "Would you believe it, she's free until four this afternoon."

Ava threw Tom his jacket. "Let's find out what she can tell us right now."

* * *

In less than half an hour, they were sitting in a waiting area outside Philippa Patterson's office. She arrived and invited them into her office. She was a petite woman dressed in billowing linen trousers and a sleeveless turtleneck jumper. Her delicate features and almond-shaped eyes reminded Ava of Audrey Hepburn, and judging by her dark brown hair, worn in Hepburn's classic *Breakfast at Tiffany's* updo, Philippa evidently liked to play on the resemblance.

"I'm responsible for finding placements for our trainee nurses. I understand you are interested in one of our ex-students, Seth Conway? Is that right?"

"Yes, ma'am," Tom Knight answered politely. "I'm afraid I can't give you any specifics, but we'd be grateful for your cooperation."

"How can I help you?" Philippa asked. Something about her manner suggested distaste for Conway. Ava had guessed right. Completely unprompted, Philippa blurted out, "Seth Conway was a deeply unpleasant young man, though he knew how to hide it very well."

Ava saw her surprise mirrored in Tom's eyes. He explained that they were particularly interested in Seth's placement at the CAMHS centre on Hope Street.

"Firstly, Seth was in no way qualified to participate in a group like that. He would have been there as an observer. The psychologist would have introduced him and asked if the group members minded him being there. It's interesting that Michaela told her mother about him, as he probably only attended a couple of her sessions. Then again, I suppose it's not that surprising. Seth was an extremely good-looking young man, oozing with charm and charisma. Seth left his nursing course not long after his placement at Hope Street. When I say 'left,' I'm being diplomatic. He started in September and was gone by Christmas. One of our female students accused him of sexual harassment outside the work place. It was her word against his and he was given the benefit of the doubt. A few weeks later, when Seth was doing a week's placement at CAMHS, I was approached by the mother of a young patient in the group Seth had been observing. She claimed that another young woman in the group had tipped her off that Seth had been approaching her daughter after her sessions and inviting her to parties. Her daughter denied it, as did Seth. He accused the other girl of jealousy — said she had a crush on him and was upset when he rejected her advances and wanted to get revenge."

"How old were these girls?" Tom interrupted. Philippa gave him a knowing smile.

"Fourteen. And emotionally vulnerable."

Ava did a quick calculation. Seth would have been in his early twenties. But it wasn't just the age difference. Seth had known the young woman was vulnerable, not least emotionally, and he had been in a position of trust.

"Once again we couldn't prove anything, of course. Though he was very much on my radar by then. There's no smoke without fire, Sergeant.

"Who was the girl?" Tom asked, sounding eager. "Was her name Michaela?"

Philippa shook her head. "I'll check my records. It was some time ago, Sergeant."

"Did Seth decide to leave the course voluntarily?" Ava asked.

Philippa smiled. "Not exactly. I had a hand in it. With a little help from my then fifteen-year-old daughter."

"You set him up?" Tom and Ava exchanged looks.

"Of course not. What sort of mother do you think I am, Sergeant Knight? I didn't have to set him up. He approached my daughter in the hospital car park, where she was waiting for me to finish work. He chatted to her for a few minutes, then stuck his hand up her skirt. My daughter was in school uniform."

Ava gasped.

"Yes. Charming character, isn't he? My daughter pushed him away and he tried to force her into the car. Fortunately my daughter has a good pair of lungs on her and her screams alerted a security guard. Seth made a big mistake." She sighed. "Even so, he got away with it, claimed he'd stumbled and fallen against my daughter and she toppled backwards into the car. He denied touching her inappropriately. They were on the wrong side of the car for the CCTV camera to show what really happened. Given the choice of believing a man who had twice before been suspected of inappropriate sexual behaviour and my daughter, I believed my daughter. I managed to 'persuade' him that he wasn't cut out to be a mental health nurse." Philippa's eyes shone with triumph. "So. Let me just see if I can find the name of the girl whose mother accused him of inappropriate behaviour at Hope Street."

Ava and Tom waited while she clattered away on her keyboard.

"Here we go. Yes, Michaela Howard."

Tom and Ava exchanged looks of satisfaction.

"I take it this name means something to you two?" Philippa looked at them with raised eyebrows.

Tom nodded. "It does, ma'am."

"Well, if he hasn't already been put away for being a sick pervert, I hope you find something to nail him for, Detectives."

Ava and Tom thanked Philippa for her time and left. They walked back to where Tom had parked at the far end of the car park. This part of the parking area had been empty when they arrived, but now it was completely full. Ava looked on, amused, while a disgruntled Tom inspected every inch of their car's paintwork.

"Jeez, Tom. Sooner or later, it's going to get a mark on it. It's not as if we're responsible for it, it's a bloody police car." Tom glared at her as though she had uttered a profanity, but all he said was, "It's a nice motor."

When she and Tom got back to the office, Ava cast PJ an enquiring look.

"It wasn't so bad," PJ assured her. "Patsy Howard's been persuaded not to blab to the press. I think the info I got about Seth Conway helped, like you said."

"Tom and I have found out a bit more. Seth Conway is a very nasty piece of work. And clever with it, so it appears. The original Teflon man." Ava told PJ what Philippa Patterson had said.

PJ nodded. "I see what you mean. Hard to believe he could get off with it every single time. He sounds like a textbook psycho, all charm on the outside, total evil bastard underneath. Bet he can go for weeks without blinking."

"Philippa's account makes it more than likely that he tried it on with Michaela Howard. Or attempted to."

Neal appeared at the door of his office. He walked over and perched on the edge of Ava's desk, signalling to Tom Knight to join them. Ava updated him and Neal nodded. He seemed eager to tell them something.

"I checked back with Ashley Hunt. The iron found in the river where Leanne Jackson's body was discovered is a match for the injury to her head, and we have confirmation that traces of her DNA were on it. The implications for our case are very positive indeed. If we can track down the artist responsible for the design on the iron, he or she might be able to provide some information on where and when it was sold — and if we're very lucky, to whom."

"Sir, does this confirm that Leanne Jackson might have been murdered on a narrowboat and was either cast overboard or jumped into the water as we thought?" Ava asked.

Ignoring her, Neal took out his phone and showed them a photograph. "Dan sent me a picture of the iron. PJ, I'll forward this to you. I'd like you to start making enquiries. See if you can identify the artist responsible for this design. Tom, in the light of the information Philippa Patterson gave you, I think we need to obtain a list of names of young people who would have come into contact with Seth Conway during his time at CAMHS. It would also be helpful to speak with anyone else who worked with Conway, including the psychologist as soon as he's available. And get someone to find a place where a boat could have been moored a mile either side of where Ruby Kennedy was found."

Turning to Ava, Neal said, "Pam Hollings phoned again earlier, asking about Jess Stokes. I think it's time we found out if Jess is caught up in all this. If she is, we need to treat her disappearance with the utmost urgency."

He didn't need to say that Jess's life could be in danger.

Chapter Sixteen

Neal and Ava were on their way to Jess's college.

"As you say, it's highly likely that the husband was responsible for the distasteful incident with the offal, but poisoning a dog is a big step up." Neal looked thoughtful. "Strange, Jock was speculating about the fate of the dog Michaela Smith tried to rescue. He seemed to think it odd that it drowned and suggested it might have been poisoned. We'll never know, as no autopsy was carried out."

Ava frowned. "What concerns me most is that Jess hinted to Pam that she was going to do some snooping of her own. What if, like Leanne, she discovered something?"

"It's unlikely," Neal said. "She wouldn't have known where to start, for one thing."

Jess might not have discovered anything, but the fact that she was making enquiries might have come to the attention of the wrong person or people. Ava wished she'd been more insistent that Jess meet her the evening she'd asked to talk.

At the college, Neal and Ava presented themselves at the main reception area, a bright and busy space milling with students and visitors. Neal had called ahead, and he moved to the front of the queue and flashed his ID at the receptionist. Ava followed him, ignoring the murmurs of complaint from people in the queue.

A young man appeared and ushered them into a corridor leading to some stairs. Upstairs, they followed him along another corridor to the Human Resources department. The students' artwork was displayed on the corridor walls. Ava looked at the paintings and photographs appreciatively. She had achieved an A grade in A level art and design and had flirted with the idea of going to art school, before deciding that it wasn't likely to lead to gainful employment. There were times when she regretted that decision.

They were left in the care of a gracious woman who introduced herself as Bijal Singh. She was expecting them and had a folder tucked under her arm with Jess Stokes' name on the front.

Bijal's office overlooked the HR floor. She closed the louvered blinds while Neal and Ava helped themselves to tea and coffee from flasks on a spare table. "Leftover from a meeting earlier," Bijal explained. "I have Jess's file here. Of course, most information is stored electronically, just depends what you want to know."

"Is it unusual for Jess to be off without contacting the college?" Neal asked.

"Most unusual, Inspector. Jess always informed us first thing in the morning if she was going to be absent from work. It's been two days now and of course we've tried to contact her, but without success. Should I be concerned, officers?" She looked from Neal to Ava.

"Not at the moment," Neal said. "What can you tell us about Jess?"

"Jess is a reliable and popular member of staff. She won a staff award last year for her exemplary work supporting our disabled students. 'Always ready to go the extra mile,' was a common comment from her students and co-workers. Jess's line manager, Trish Eaton, said Jess has really grown in confidence since starting work at the college a couple of years ago. Actually, you'd probably be better off speaking with Trish. She knows Jess better than I do." Bijal consulted her watch. "Trish has made herself available for the next hour or so. Shall I give her a buzz and ask her to come over?"

"Perhaps you could direct us to Ms Eaton instead?" Neal suggested.

Bijal nodded and picked up the phone on her desk. "Colin, can you pop into my office, please." She hung up and said, "Our latest apprentice, bless him. He'll take you over. He won't be a minute."

Before she'd finished speaking, there was a knock at her door and a young man dressed in a Black Watch tartan suit and pointy leather brogues entered the room.

Bijal pulled up her blinds. "That's better. Hate being stuck in here by myself." She gave a wave to someone below. *She's a people person,* Ava thought.

Without uttering a word, Colin led them back along the corridor, down the stairs and out into the main part of the college campus.

"Nice suit," Ava commented.

"Black Watch," Neal said, to be met with a vacant look from Colin. "The tartan. It's called Black Watch. Scottish regimental tartan."

Colin muttered something that sounded like, "Yeah?"

"I knew that," Ava whispered to Neal.

Colin led them to a door and stepped back. "This is it."

He showed no inclination to knock, so Ava stepped forward and tapped lightly, while Neal gave Colin much exaggerated thanks. Sarcasm's wasted on this one, she thought.

Trish was a breath of fresh air after the surly Colin. She was looking concerned. "Please tell me nothing bad's happened to Jess."

"We have no reason to believe so at the present time," Neal answered. He was being professional, not uncaring, Ava knew.

Neal went through a list of routine questions about Jess's character, her work record, whether she had seemed worried about anything. They learned again what a likeable, caring individual Jess was, how she was a bit unconfident but wonderful at her job. Neal turned to the subject of Leanne Jackson's murder.

"Jess was upset the morning after that happened," Trish said. "She told me that she'd gone to the riverside to see where the poor woman's body was recovered. She knew Leanne Jackson at school, apparently."

A bell sounded outside. Trish excused herself, saying that she had a class to take. She opened the door to the corridor which was already filling with students in transit. One of them, a burly young man, made a beeline for Ava and gave her a bear hug.

Trish boomed out, "Barney! How do we say hello to someone we don't know?"

"Pleased to meet you," Barney said, and thrust out his hand. Ava shook it. Trish had to remind him to let go.

"Please excuse Barney, Sergeant. He tends to get carried away sometimes." Trish lowered her voice. "He has a weakness for pretty young women."

"No worries," Ava assured her, smiling.

They left the building and crossed the campus to the car park. Like the university, Stromford's college seemed to be ever-expanding, taking over or erecting buildings all over the place. You could hardly move for students in certain parts of town these days. Ava thought of her own, brief experience of being a student and the sudden tragedy that had caused her to drop out. It was a scar in her life that she had shared with few people. Maggie Neal was one of them. Ava hoped she hadn't told Neal.

He turned to her. "You're worried about Jess, aren't you?"

"What? Oh, yes. I can't help thinking she's got herself mixed up in all of this somehow. But I can't believe that she found anything to put her in danger. She didn't have the time to do more than make a few enquiries at the college. There's all that business with the dog, too. I'm pretty sure Michael Hollings planted the organs, but I can't believe he had anything to do with poisoning Pam's dog. Maybe it was someone trying to warn Jess off, you know, by hurting someone close to her? Then there's Pam's mugging."

"Hmm. Threatening someone's loved ones is a more effective strategy than making a direct threat to the person themselves. Did Jess give any indication that she'd been threatened?"

"No. But when she called, I got a distinct impression that there was more she wanted to tell me, but not over the phone."

"Was she in a relationship?" Neal asked.

"I think so, but we didn't really get around to talking about that. Obviously we'll need to check him out."

"Let's swing by Jess's place now," Neal said.

"Okay, sir."

* * *

It was a short drive from the college to Jess's flat. Ava had called ahead, and Pam Hollings was watching out for them at an upstairs window. She disappeared from view and then reappeared at the entrance door.

"Thank you for coming. I'm frantic with worry about Jess. This makes what happened to Bunty pale in comparison." As they stepped over the threshold, Ava couldn't help picturing the poor dog lying there. Pam showed them into Jess's flat. The rooms all seemed undisturbed, until they reached the kitchen.

Ava was immediately struck by the sight of Jess's familiar blue and white striped swimsuit lying on the floor. It was one of a number of items that appeared to have 'fallen off' a clothes horse set up next to a radiator. A brief glance passed between Ava and Neal, unseen by Pam, who tutted and bent to pick them up. Ava grabbed her arm and pulled her back.

The heap of clothes was just one of many signs that something was amiss. The fridge door was ajar. A door leading down a step to what seemed to be a large pantry was wide open. The kettle was standing by the sink instead of on its base. All indicated a scuffle, someone taken by surprise.

Pam caught on quickly. "Jess wouldn't leave her things on the floor like that. She looked after her clothes." Her eyes darted around the room and her hand went to her mouth. "Oh God. Something's happened to Jess. I knew it. I should have come down and had a look around sooner."

"It's good that you didn't, Mrs Hollings," Neal said. "If there's any forensic evidence here it will be easier for us to find if Jess's flat has been undisturbed."

"Forensic evidence? You mean like . . . blood?"

"Please don't upset yourself, Mrs Hollings. There's no real evidence of violence here." Neal's soft Scottish accent had its customary calming effect. Pam nodded, seemingly reassured. She hadn't seen what Ava had just spied on one of the kitchen table legs. A smear of blood. She stepped in front of it to hide it from Pam, earning a grateful nod from Neal.

"Come and sit down in the other room," Ava urged, gently nudging Pam out of the kitchen and into the hallway. Neal already had his mobile out and was arranging for forensics to come round.

"Who else has keys to Jess's flat besides you, Mrs Hollings?" Ava asked.

"No one. Unless . . . Mitch . . . Mitchell West. He's Jess's boyfriend."

"Have you met him?" Ava asked.

Pam shook her head. "They haven't been together very long. He's a fireman. He hasn't stayed here much. I wouldn't have thought she'd have given him a key yet. We cut keys for each other because we're friends and . . . and because of Bunty. Jess used to take her for walks if I wasn't around. Magda has a boyfriend, but I don't know his name. He's Polish, like Magda."

"What about your ex-husband?" Ava asked gently.

"Absolutely not." Her horrified expression said it all. Then she closed her eyes for a moment. "Oh no. I've just remembered. Jess and Mitch had a row a couple of nights ago. Apparently Jess had coffee with another man. What if. .?

"Young couples have rows all the time. It doesn't necessarily mean anything," Ava said. Nevertheless, she was keen to interview Mitch West as soon as she could.

With a wan smile, Pam got to her feet. "I'll let you get on now. Will you call on me before you leave? I'll be upstairs in my flat. Let me know if there's anything I can help you with."

Ava thanked Pam. She closed the door behind her, and as she turned, she caught her hair on the button of a jacket hanging on a hook on the door. She recognised the jacket. It was the one Jess was wearing when Ava had last seen her at the pool. While she was disentangling her hair, she noticed a piece of paper sticking out of the pocket. She pulled it out and ran her eyes over the handwritten message.

"Sir!" she cried. "You need to take a look at this."

Ava handed Neal the note. His eyebrows rose. "No name, obviously," he said.

Ava put it in an evidence bag. "It makes me wonder if it's a warning rather than a threat. I mean it could be someone who didn't want her to be harmed. Or someone who cared about her, warning her off. Pam just told me that Jess and her boyfriend had a row a couple of nights ago . . ." She looked at Neal.

Neal nodded. "She might have confided in a boyfriend, or someone she was close to. Who else might know she was asking questions, other than Pam and the people at the college?"

Ava sighed. "I don't know who else Pam might have spoken to. Or Jess." She cocked an ear and went to the window. She saw a man and a strange-looking dog walking up the path to the door.

Ava frowned. "I'll just see who that is."

Pam was halfway down the stairs when Ava opened Jess's door.

"It's my friend, Henry Bolt. I hope you don't mind, I asked him to come over." Pam's face was flushed, and Ava guessed that Henry was more than just a friend.

"Boris!" Pam exclaimed. It took Ava a moment to realise she was addressing the dog.

Henry was less enthusiastic. He seemed keen to go on upstairs.

Before Ava had a chance to ask, Pam said, "I've told Henry everything, DS Merry. Henry's been a tower of strength since I lost Bunty."

Ava spotted forensics pulling up outside and excused herself. She made a mental note to add Henry Bolt to her list of people to check up on.

"Hey, Ava."

Ava smiled at Dan Cardew. "Hey, Dan. How's Faye?" On their last case, a young forestry worker had shown an interest in Dan, and rumour had it that she and Dan were now an item.

Dan grinned. "I'm seeing her later, actually."

Neal looked up when they entered the kitchen.

"I think we're looking at a crime scene here." He sounded weary. "It's possible a young woman has been abducted. There's evidence of a scuffle and one visible smear of blood on the leg of the table there." Dan scanned the room with a practised eye. "There's also this." Neal handed him the bag containing the handwritten note.

They heard a loud voice coming from the hallway. "What the hell's going on? Where's Jess?"

Ava put her head round the kitchen door and saw a young man striding towards her. "Mitch?" she asked. He nodded, straining to see past her into the kitchen. "I'm Detective Sergeant Ava Merry."

The man turned pale. "Oh no! Jess. .."

Ava took him by the arm and propelled him back along the hallway into the living room, where she pushed him gently but firmly onto the sofa. She was getting good at this. "Take some deep breaths," she ordered.

But he was already struggling to his feet. "Is she. .? Is Jess. .?

"The short answer is, we don't know. Jess has been missing for a couple of days. Her neighbour was worried." *And she's not the only one,* thought Ava.

Neal joined them. He looked closely at Mitch. "When did you last see Jess Stokes?"

"Two nights ago. Surely you don't think . . .?"

"Jess's neighbour told us that you and Jess had a row, something about her having coffee with another man," Neal said.

Mitch shook his head slowly from side to side. "I behaved like a jealous kid. I've been trying to get in touch with Jess since yesterday to apologise, but the calls have been going straight to voicemail."

"We'll need you to account for your whereabouts in the past two days Mr . . .?" Neal said.

"West. Mitchell West. I'm a fireman. I've been working practically non-stop. You can check my shifts. I came round now to apologise to Jess and take her out for pizza." He rubbed at his chin. "Have you contacted Jess's mum and dad? Maybe she's just gone home for a couple of days."

"She didn't go home," Ava said. It occurred to her that Mitch probably didn't know what had happened since his row with Jess. She explained about Bunty and the other incidents, and watched his anger mount.

"You need to be round questioning that ex-husband of Pam's. He's the one who's responsible. I should have gone round myself. I could have stopped him." Mitch made to stand up.

"That would have been unwise." Neal said. "Mr Hollings is being questioned at the moment."

Ava nodded. Given what they knew, it seemed unlikely that a jealous ex-husband could be their man, but Mitch needed to clutch at something.

* * *

Michael Hollings lived in a village five miles north of the city. "He works from home," PJ told Tom. "Music teacher. Piano and violin. The DI plays piano, doesn't he? I've heard he's pretty good." They were sitting in a queue of cars waiting to pass some roadworks.

"Oh yeah? Thought the bagpipes would be more his style."

PJ glared at him. "Oh, I get it. You've got the hots for Ava."

Tom grinned. "So, how do you rate my chances?"

PJ gave a snort.

"What? You think Ava's out of my league?"

"It's not that . . ." PJ stalled. She'd overheard a conversation in the ladies loo the night of Ava's birthday drinks in which Tom Knight had been compared with Bradley Cooper. She wasn't about to share that with him.

Tom stared at her. "What then? I know she's not seeing anyone at the moment, so what's the problem?"

The problem, PJ thought, is that Ava belongs with Neal, and Neal with Ava. PJ had known this even when she fancied Neal herself. Unfortunately, it was all too easy to see Ava hooking up with someone like Tom. She kept her feelings for Neal buried deep inside her and when it came to affairs of the heart, Neal, bless him, was so backward at coming forward that he'd die of a broken heart before he went digging. The pair of them needed a good kicking. PJ stared gloomily at Tom's handsome profile. Bradley Cooper. Oh boy.

"Left at the junction," she snapped. They were moving again.

They drove the rest of the way in silence, broken only by PJ's barked directions. Tom made a sharp turn into a cul-de-sac and slowed in front of a large stone house. "This is it," PJ announced. They walked up the garden path. The sound of piano music grew louder as they neared the porch. "Chopin," PJ said. Tom looked at her. "What, you thought I wouldn't know any classical music?"

They had to ring twice. "He's finishing the piece," PJ said, pacing impatiently. When Michael Hollings finally appeared, he made no apology, but he did invite them in. He showed them into a small sitting room. PJ was glad he hadn't offered coffee; she'd caught a glimpse of the kitchen in passing. It looked as though he hadn't cleared up in there for weeks.

Hollings waved an arm. "Excuse the scant décor. My wife took all the best furniture with her when she moved into that ghastly little flat. Stole it, really. I wasn't in at the time. My neighbour saw a transit van in the driveway, and Pamela letting two men into the house." He sniffed. "At least she didn't clear me out completely."

PJ looked around. The room seemed well enough furnished to her.

"So, what is she accusing me of now? I assume that's why you're here. Pamela claims I've been slapping her around again. Am I right?" His tone was mocking. Pam hadn't mentioned anything about her husband being abusive. Nice of Hollings to volunteer the information.

"Have you?" Tom asked.

Hollings sighed. "Here we go again. My wife decides she wants a divorce and she thinks the easiest way to ensure she gets the lot is to accuse me of being a wife beater. When will you people learn that there are two sides to every story?"

PJ consulted her watch. "We're in no hurry, Mr Hollings. There's ample time for us to hear your side of it." PJ tried hard to be fair, but Michael Hollings's arrogance made it difficult.

"Mr Hollings?" she said.

Hollings seemed to come out of a reverie. "Just why are you here, Detectives?"

"We're here as part of our investigation into the disappearance of your wife's neighbour, Jess Stokes," Tom said.

Michael Hollings sounded confused and angry. "What the hell's that got to do with me? I've never even met her."

Tom looked at him. "Jess hasn't been seen for a couple of days. Before she disappeared there had been a couple of incidents. Your wife was mugged, for one thing. What can you tell us about that?"

"Pam was mugged? Jesus, was she hurt?"

Tom was curt. "She's fine. Answer the question."

"I . . . didn't know until you told me just now. Surely you can't think I had anything to do with it?"

"Tell us what you know about your wife's dog being killed," Tom continued.

"Bunty? Bunty's dead?"

"She was poisoned," said Tom. "Do you have anything to say?"

"Bunty? Are you serious? My wife thought more of that dog than she did of me. I can't believe the mutt was out of her sight long enough to get itself poisoned." PJ gave him a long, cold stare. "Oh, I get it. Pamela thinks it was me. She probably poisoned the bloody animal herself and set me up for it. And no doubt you lot will believe her over anything I have to say. Whatever happened to innocent before proven guilty?"

PJ sighed. "No one's accused you of anything, Mr Hollings."

"It's the implication," Hollings whined.

"There was an earlier incident," Tom continued. "Concerning a bag of organs."

Hollings seemed to deliberate. Finally he said, "Alright, so I admit to planting the offal under the stairs. It was only a harmless prank."

"Hardly harmless. It upset your wife's neighbours when they found it. Not to mention the amount of police time wasted on establishing that the organs were animal in origin."

"That should have been obvious! I got them down the bloody butchers for God's sake."

"I think you were trying to intimidate your ex-wife."

"My wife," Hollings corrected Tom. "Pamela and I are not yet divorced."

"Excuse me, your wife, then."

"No . . . I . . . okay it was bloody stupid of me, but I didn't kill the dog," Hollings blurted. "I wouldn't do that. I'm not a bloody monster." PJ wasn't so sure. "I gave her the bloody dog. Cost a fortune. Pedigree as long as your arm."

"Did you take Bunty's collar?"

"I . . . er . . . yes. I happened to be on the west common and saw Bunty trapped by the collar . . ." He was winging it by now.

"You were stalking her," PJ said.

"If there's any forensic evidence to link you with Bunty's poisoning, our people will find it. In the meantime, I'd advise you to stay away from your wife, Mr Hollings."

Tom was about to wind up the interview when PJ's phone pinged. She showed him Ava's message.

"Does the name Seth Conway mean anything to you, Mr Hollings?" asked Tom. Hollings looked blank. "We'll just take a quick look around, Mr Hollings, and then we'll be on our way."

Hollings gave them a sour look. "Look away, Sergeant. You won't find any missing women here. I'll be in my music room."

PJ spent the next half hour listening to Chopin's nocturnes, while Tom searched the house. He found nothing.

Michael Hollings's music followed them all the way to their car. PJ wondered how it was that a scumbag like Michael Hollings could create such beautiful music. But at least their visit had confirmed one thing. Jess Stokes wasn't at his house.

Chapter Seventeen

Ava drove home from Jess's flat with a heavy heart. She opened the door and a rich aroma assailed her. Ollie had been cooking.

"Casserole in the oven," he called, "but you'll need to reheat it."

"Ollie, you're a marvel. I'm starving. How's the studying going?"

"Good. No time to talk." Ollie spoke abruptly, but Ava smiled, unoffended. Ollie wasn't always in the mood to be sociable and he was seldom subtle in his dealings with people. Sometimes Ava had to remind him to consider what effect his words might have on others.

She left him to it and went into the kitchen where she removed her meal from the oven and stuck it in the microwave. Ollie wouldn't approve. In ten minutes she was sitting on the sofa, her meal on her lap, watching Lex Thorner on YouTube. The music wasn't as bad as she'd expected, despite the awful sound quality. Unsurprisingly, the cameras were all focused on the singer. She was watching her third video when a change of tempo in the music brought people onto the dance floor. Maybe now she would be able to see the attendees. Ava leaned forward and peered at the dancers. They were mostly women, all ages, shapes and sizes, and in all stages of sobriety. The camera panned around the room, pausing briefly at a group of women who were waving at the camera. One young man waved both arms and stood up to do a little dance. Two men sat at his table, seemingly engaged in a heated conversation. Ava stared at them, and an idea formed in her head. She set the remains of her meal aside and reached for her phone.

"Ava?" Neal answered immediately.

"Sir, I think I might have a lead on finding Seth Conway."

"Go on."

"Do you remember the young man we met at the college when we were speaking with Jess Stokes's manager, Trish?"

"Yes, I remember. He took quite a shine to you. His name was Barney, wasn't it? What about him? You're not going to tell me he's mixed up in all this?"

"He was at Jeffers the night Mac's brother was performing there. Two men were with him. One of them was Seth Conway, and the other looked like a family member, possibly a brother. I think it would be worth bringing him in for questioning."

Silence. Neal was probably weighing up the possibilities. Ava wondered if she were clutching at straws. She was still blaming herself for Jess's disappearance. If she had only insisted that Jess meet with her that evening . . .

At last Neal spoke. "Nice work, Ava. I think we should follow it up in the morning, though. I don't like the idea of upsetting that young man at this hour."

"But, sir. Jess . . . Yes, sir." Maybe Neal was right. Maybe what she had seen was just a coincidence. But Ava was convinced it was more than that. She ran the scene again and was sure that the two men with Barney were more than casual acquaintances. She glanced at the time. Okay, Neal was right.

Ava sighed, knowing she wouldn't sleep that night. She was right. She lay awake bouncing the multifarious strands of the investigation around in her head until she finally fell into a restless doze. She dreamt that everyone involved in the case were together on the dance floor at Jeffers Club, moving slowly around like figures on a chessboard.

As soon as she reached work the following morning, she called the college and asked to speak to Jess's line manager, Trish Eaton.

"Barney's surname is Cole," said Trish. "He's staying in an assisted living unit. His brother Jonty would likely have accompanied him to a club like that. He has Barney over to stay a lot and often takes him out. If you don't mind my asking, why are you so interested in Barney, Sergeant Merry?"

Ava ignored this. "Was Jess one of Barney's support workers?"

"Have you found Jess? Is she okay?"

"Jess is still missing. We're following up some leads on people she might have associated with. Did Jess know Barney's brother, Jonty?"

"Yes, we all know Jonty. He drops his brother off a couple of times a week. Lovely young man. I've seen him chatting to Jess quite a bit just recently . . . Oh dear, you're not thinking Jonty . . ."

"Not at all, Mrs Eaton, and I'd be grateful if you'd keep this conversation between the two of us, please. Is this one of Jonty's mornings for dropping his brother off, do you know?"

"Yes, it is, actually. He should be here in half an hour or so. He usually drops Barney off early."

Ava looked at her watch. She could be there in ten minutes.

She jogged round to the college, thinking about Trish Eaton's words, 'I've seen him chatting to Jess quite a bit just recently.' She waited opposite the entrance to the building and, as luck would have it, Jonty was early this morning. Ava saw Barney first and hoped he wouldn't notice her. She was standing in the smoking shelter and had pulled her hood up to conceal her face. The man with Barney was tall but stooped, the way shy people often were. Ava guessed he was in his early twenties.

She waited until he had said goodbye to his brother and was on his way back to the car park before she called out to him. "Jonty Cole?"

He stopped and nodded.

"I'm Detective Sergeant Ava Merry. I'd like to ask you a couple of questions about Jess Stokes. She's one of Barney's support workers, isn't she?"

"Yeah, I know Jess." Was she imagining it, or did he seem wary?

"Are you aware that Jess hasn't been seen for a few days? We have some concerns about her safety."

"Oh."

"You don't know where she might be?"

"No. Why should I? Is Jess okay?"

"How well do you know a man by the name of Seth Conway?"

At the mention of Seth's name, Jonty spun around and ran.

Ava was so surprised that for a few seconds she could only stand and stare after him. "Shit." She began to sprint after him, closing the distance between them fast, but not quite fast enough. She caught him up just in time to bang on the roof of his car as it moved forward, the engine screaming. "Shit, shit, shit, shit, shit!" Ava made a note of the registration number but didn't need it. Cole's car came to a standstill as soon as it hit the early-morning traffic on the main road.

Jonty made an attempt to edge out and jump the queue but he didn't stand a chance, so he did exactly what Ava expected him to do and bolted again. He swung open his car door and legged it, leaving his vehicle in the road.

This time, she was ready. Her gruelling fitness routine meant that Ava could run for miles, though Jonty gave her a good run for her money. He wove through the throng of startled commuters and reached the city's busiest road junction. He glanced over his shoulder at Ava, hot on his heels, and plunged on, heedless of the oncoming traffic. Ava charged after him amidst a chorus of blaring horns and the shouts of angry motorists.

Then, suddenly, it was all over. A couple of community PCs appeared out of nowhere and Jonty ran straight into them. Ava ran up, whipped out her ID and cautioned him.

She beamed at them. "Great timing, guys!"

"You can't arrest me," Jonty gasped. "I haven't done anything wrong."

"Then why did you run?" Ava asked. She gave a nod, and one of the officers cuffed him.

"Want us to bring him down to the station?" he asked.

Within twenty minutes, Jonty was sweating it out in one of the interview rooms, while Ava accounted for her late arrival at work.

PJ shook her head. "And I thought you'd just slept in. Should have known better."

Neal smiled at her. "Good work, Ava."

The interview with Jonty Cole had to wait until after the morning meeting. Tom Knight had spoken with the psychologist from CAHMS whose sessions Chantelle Clarke and Michaela Smith had attended. The psychologist, Dr Jean Rowlands, remembered Michaela Howard's mother making a complaint against Seth during his time at Hope Street, but there had been insufficient evidence to warrant an investigation.

"How the hell Conway managed to get himself a position at the Yeardsley Trust is a total mystery," intoned Tom. "There's no way they could have checked his background. It's bloody scandalous."

Neal nodded. "And as we know, all too common." Ava was muttering expletives, while PJ shook her head.

"I also discovered that Leanne Jackson had been in touch with Dr Rowlands only weeks before her death." They all stared at Tom.

"Didn't she think to contact us when Leanne's body was found?" Ava asked.

"She's just back from a sabbatical in the States. She missed the news about Leanne's death. Shame. If she'd stayed at home, we might have got to this point a bit sooner."

"What did they discuss?" Neal asked.

"Leanne was after information on Conway. Dr Rowlands also confirmed that she knew Leanne from her time at CAMHS. Remember Tina Jackson mentioned something about Leanne attending what she termed, 'anger management?'" They nodded. "Well, it wasn't quite that. It was a group for troubled teens whose problems had resulted in difficult behaviours."

"So Leanne knew Seth Conway years ago?" Neal said.

"Yes, sir. She was in one or more of his sessions."

"That's mega, Tom," Ava exclaimed. "We now have a direct connection between Seth Conway and Leanne Jackson. Possible motive, the works. I mean, Seth might have been abusing Leanne as well, right? She contacts Ruby Kennedy, another possible victim of Seth's, with a view to getting her to come forward as well, Seth gets wind of this and kills them both to keep them quiet."

PJ and Tom were nodding, but Neal's expression was inscrutable.

"What changed her mind about coming forward before, I wonder?" Neal said. "I mean, she could have told the police years ago. It might have kept her out of prison."

"I think Leanne was acting on behalf of the others," PJ said quietly. "Maybe it wasn't until she came across Chantelle and Michaela's names at the Trust and thought about their deaths. She might have realised that they might well be a direct result of Seth's abuse. I mean, their mental health was already fragile. Suppose Chantelle took pills because she couldn't live with it any longer. Maybe Michaela felt the same way. Maybe she jumped into the river after the dog because she didn't really care whether she came back out alive. Maybe Leanne felt responsible when she heard about it. It gave her a wake-up call."

It was the most likely explanation, Ava thought.

"Where are we on tracking down the witness to Michaela's drowning?" Neal asked.

"We've got the statement sir," Tom said, "But we're having trouble contacting the witness. It seems that he's moved away and we're still trying to contact him."

Everyone understood the implications of this. If the witness was deemed unreliable, it might confirm that they had three murders on their hands. It might never be possible to say for certain that Chantelle's death wasn't a suicide, but Ava was convinced that directly or not, Seth Conway was responsible.

"Alright. Good work, Tom. The pieces are starting to fall into place." Neal nodded to PJ, who had been tasked with contacting the other women in the group.

"I spoke with Alyssa Ballard's mother via Skype. They moved to Australia, right? When I mentioned Seth's name, I thought she must have cut me off because there was one of those long silences. Finally she said," PJ read aloud from her notebook, "'I knew this business would come back to haunt us. If I'd had my way that man would have been put inside years ago, but the girls — Chantelle and Michaela, as well as my Alyssa — wouldn't say a word against him. He was as slippery as an eel, that one, always coming up with some convincing story. That's why we moved here. To make a fresh start.'"

PJ put her notebook aside. "Mrs Ballard put me in touch with Alyssa, and she confirmed that Leanne had contacted her recently, sir. She wanted Alyssa to make a statement confirming that she had been a victim of historical abuse. This was a week before Leanne died. Alyssa had agreed to make a statement. She was shocked to hear about Leanne and Ruby and wants to give evidence when we nail Seth Conway."

"Thanks, everyone." Neal said, "So, to summarise, this is what we now know: while on a placement at CAMHS, trainee mental health nurse Seth Conway sees an opportunity to abuse vulnerable young women. He gets away with it through a combination of his charm and the girls' reluctance to testify against him. He is thrown off his course because he makes a stupid mistake and assaults the daughter of his mentor. Again, he gets away with it. Incidentally, I checked and Seth had intended to specialise in child and adolescent mental health."

"Hmm," Tom said. "Typical of a paedophile to choose a career that provides opportunities to feed his sick obsession. But kids with mental health problems — that's got to be the lowest of the low."

Neal continued. "We don't know if Leanne was one of Seth's victims. At the Yeardsley Trust she discovers that two former Trust attendees, Chantelle and Michaela, have died in unusual circumstances and she becomes obsessed — we know that Leanne was an obsessive individual — with finding out what happened to the other young women that she knew from those therapy sessions. Maybe she thinks memories of their abuse pushed these women over the edge. She contacts Ruby Kennedy and somehow the two of them end up in Seth's murderous clutches. Now we know that Alyssa Ballard was abused, it's a fair bet that the woman we've yet to trace — Corinna Masters — was also one of Seth's victims." Neal became aware of the others staring at him and he realised he'd been drumming his fingers on his desk as he spoke. He stopped abruptly and turned to another matter.

"Yesterday afternoon, Ava and I visited Jess Stokes's flat. As you know, she's been missing for a couple of days now. There were signs of a scuffle, perhaps more than that. I think we can now assume that Jess Stokes is connected with our current investigation, and that Seth Conway might have abducted her." There was no need for him to add that Jess might be dead already.

"How did Leanne locate the bastard?" Tom said, angrily.

How indeed? All their efforts so far had come up with nothing. It was as though Seth Conway had disappeared off the face of the earth. He had no doubt reinvented himself, and was living under a new name. One thing was certain. He would still be abusing teenage girls, which on the face of it, should make it easier to find him. He would be the youth worker, or the schoolteacher, or the children's nurse. The one with the friendly face, who invited trust and betrayed it in the cruellest way, by stealing their innocence.

"Ava? You okay?" PJ had been watching Ava, who was twisting her hair tighter and tighter into a coiled pleat.

Ava let go her hair. "I'm fine. Cases like this . . . men like this . . . they just . . . get to me, that's all."

"They get to us all," Tom said quietly.

"Ava, contact Alyssa Ballard again. See if Leanne said anything to her that might give us a clue as to Conway's whereabouts. As I was saying, along with locating Seth Conway, finding Jess Stokes is now a priority. I'm releasing her details to the press today and I've already organised for uniform to do a door-to-door with neighbours and around the local area." Neal looked at PJ. "I'd be grateful if you'd pass on the names of Jess's boyfriend and the male friends of her neighbours and make sure they're included. And carry on with the search for Corinna Masters. We're making good progress on this case, folks. Keep at it. It's dogged work, I know, but that's mostly what police work is all about. If you're in it for the excitement, you're going to be disappointed ninety per cent of the time."

PJ smiled at this, but Tom and Ava were expressionless. Neal suspected that Tom, like Ava, craved a bit of action now and again.

The meeting ended.

Neal turned to Ava. "Ready for our chat with Mr Cole?"

Chapter Eighteen

Jonty had had plenty of time to think. The minute Ava and Neal walked into the interview room, he said, "I don't know where Jess is. I'd never hurt her. I've been looking out for her."

"Looking out for her? Why?" Neal asked. "Do you have reason to believe someone means her harm?"

Jonty looked at Ava. "Seth Conway, that's who."

Earlier in her career, Ava would practically have jumped out of her seat at a revelation like this. As it was, she stared straight at Jonty without showing the slightest hint of surprise. Or so she hoped.

"Seth Conway? What's your relationship with Seth Conway?" Ava asked. Jonty put his head in his hands. "I think we'd better start at the beginning, Jonty, don't you? How long have you known Seth?"

Jonty sighed. "We met when I was sixteen. At a group I used to go to. I had some . . . problems when I was younger and they sent me for therapy. Seth was one of the people who ran the group."

Ava glanced at Neal, knowing he must be thinking the same as her. Neither of them reacted.

"Why were you there, Jonty, if you don't mind me asking?" Ava said.

Jonty looked defensive. "I was referred for counselling."

She nodded. "Okay. So this was what? Six, seven years ago? How old are you now, Jonty?"

"Twenty-four." Eight years ago.

"And what? You remained in contact? You were friends?" Ava asked.

Jonty stared at his hands. "Yeah. To start with, anyway."

"Seth was quite a bit older than you, wasn't he? What was he, a bit like a big brother to you? Mind you, I would have thought that his professional relationship with you would prevent him seeing you outside of your therapy sessions, or is that not the case?" Ava raised an eyebrow.

"It was after he left. Seth wasn't there for long. He was only doing a training placement there or something."

"Did he contact you after he left?" Ava asked.

"Yeah." Jonty looked at Neal pleadingly.

"Go on, son," Neal said gently. "Did he get in touch with you for a particular reason?"

"I . . . it was . . . it was the girls. He wanted to know about some of the girls in my counselling sessions." Ava caught her breath. The atmosphere in the room was electric.

"Before I say any more, I need to know that Barney will be safe." Jonty had tears in his eyes.

Neal frowned. "Why wouldn't your brother be safe, Jonty?"

"Seth . . . Seth said . . . He said he'd hurt Barney if I ever told anyone." Jonty sniffed and wiped his cheeks.

Neal gave him a minute. "Tell us what you know and we'll guarantee Barney's safety," he assured Jonty.

Jonty cleared his throat. "To begin with, he was a mate. I was going through a bad time. The other kids at school used to take the piss out of me because of Barney."

Ava noticed how unconfident Jonty seemed. "I never used to go anywhere without him. My mum sort of left me to look after him a lot when he was little. She was on her own and she had to work. Our dad left when Barney was three. He couldn't cope with having a disabled kid. I didn't mind. Everyone used to say how good I was with him."

Jonty looked up, as if for reassurance. Ava felt a sudden wave of pity for him and gave him an encouraging nod. She knew how it was to feel responsible for a sibling who was a little different. Though Ollie had never been given a diagnosis, she guessed he was somewhere on the autistic spectrum.

"Barney wasn't hard work, not really. But I got fed up with him always tagging along. I just wanted to have a normal life like everybody else my age. I didn't want to be Barney's carer. My mum was always asking me to 'look after Barney for a bit.' She'd say to keep an eye on Barney while she did this or that chore. But I seemed to spend longer and longer 'keeping an eye on Barney,' while my mum seemed to find more and more things to keep her busy. Don't get me wrong. Mum had problems too. She was . . . depressed, though she didn't know it at the time. Everyone commented on what a wonderful brother I was, how I was so good with Barney. So patient. I spent hours showing Barney how to dress himself. How to ride his bike with stabilisers." A small smile. "But even I couldn't get him off them. And I was the only one who could calm Barney down when he kicked off. I'd watch Thomas the Tank Engine or play trains with him for hours."

Ava glanced at Neal. She saw that he, too, was moved by Jonty's story. Still, they needed to get him to talk about Seth.

"Like I said, it was harder when I hit my teens. You know how it can be at that age, you're so bloody sensitive about how you look to your peers. Girls were especially unkind, some of them. I had low self-esteem, I started self-harming . . . . To cut a long story short, Seth talked to me about it all and he helped me understand better. He seemed like a good mate . . . back then."

Ava nodded. This fitted the picture they had of Seth.

"Why did Seth threaten to hurt your brother, Jonty? What did he want you to keep quiet about?" Ava pressed, but gently.

She had a sudden thought. Had all Jonty's talk about Barney and presenting himself as a victim been intended to soften them up? To provide a mitigating context for some greater crime? If she'd learned one thing in police work, it was not to be blindsided by a sob story.

A prolonged silence followed her question, and extended into several minutes. Long enough for Jonty to put his narrative together. Ava watched him closely. He was a big guy whose shyness and nervousness made him appear smaller than he was. It struck her suddenly that he was mimicking his brother Barney a little. Barney, too, was big, but childlike and vulnerable. Disarming.

"You need to talk to us, Jonty," Neal said.

"I . . . it was all about the girls," Jonty said. "He threatened to hurt Barney if I told anyone about the parties." Now they were getting somewhere. Ava leaned forward in her seat.

"Come on, Jonty," Neal said, impatience in his tone now. "What girls? What parties? Nobody threatens to hurt people over ordinary parties, son. So what are we really talking about here?"

"I didn't think I was doing anything wrong, at first," Jonty said pleadingly. There it was again. The little boy lost.

"Seth said he had a friend who was having a party and I could come. He suggested I ask two or three of the girls in my therapy group along. It sounded like a bit of fun, you know. He said he'd get some beers."

"These girls he asked you to bring along, they were what, fourteen, fifteen at the time? Didn't it strike you as a bit strange that someone Seth's age was asking you to invite girls that age to a party? Girls whom I'm assuming had 'issues,' as they were receiving counselling."

"It does now, but not at the time. Seth didn't seem that much older. He was a mate and we all thought he was . . . cool. The girls who came along, they all fancied him."

"What happened at these parties? Did Seth have sex with the girls? Were there other men involved?" Neal said.

Jonty twitched and fiddled with his watch strap. "Yes," he said at last. "To both questions." He looked at Neal imploringly. "It didn't seem like such a big deal at the time, I didn't realise it was wrong. We were all drunk, having fun. There was no . . . coercion. The girls didn't seem to mind having sex with Seth. He was good-looking and, like I said, they all fancied him. It didn't seem like . . . like they were being raped or anything." Jonty raised his hands. "I know. I know. I was fifteen, and that's how it seemed to me then. I know better now." Sixteen, Ava thought. She was beginning to find Jonty's repeated denials of responsibility a little hard to swallow.

"How often did Seth hold these parties? And how long were you involved in them?"

"I don't know. I went along three, maybe four times."

Ava frowned. "And Seth has been in touch with you more recently than eight years ago? When did he threaten to hurt Barney?"

"It was because of . . . of Leanne, you know, that woman who was found in the river."

"Leanne Jackson?" Ava asked. Jonty nodded. "You knew her from CAMHS?" Another nod. "Did Leanne go to these parties you were telling us about?"

"Yes."

"And she contacted you? About Seth? Did she want you to tell the police about Seth abusing underage girls?" Ava asked.

"We met a few times. I liked Leanne," he said, his lips trembling. "I used to talk to her about Barney." He'd fancied her. It occurred to Ava that Barney wasn't the only one who benefitted from their relationship. Jonty wasn't above using his brother to elicit attention from women. They would probably see him as unthreatening and compassionate. Jonty had taken his brother to Jeffers. It was unlikely that it had been for Barney's entertainment alone.

Jonty looked down. "Leanne was a good person. She didn't deserve to end up like that."

"And just to clarify, Leanne told you of her suspicions about the fate of some of the girls who'd been at CAMHS at the same time as the two of you?"

Jonty mumbled, "Yes."

"Leanne, Chantelle Clarke, Michaela Smith, Ruby Kennedy. These women are all dead, Jonty. Didn't it occur to you to come to us with the information you had on Seth?" Ava pinched herself. "That's when he got in touch with you and threatened Barney."

"I . . . heard about Chantelle . . . and . . . and . . . Michaela. But I thought Leanne was being stupid. They both topped themselves, didn't they? No one murdered them." This lack of empathy for Chantelle and Michaela seemed oddly at variance with the stories he'd just told them about being so caring.

"I changed my mind when I heard about Leanne and Ruby. Seth knew Leanne had contacted me. I don't know anything else." His voice rose.

"Actually, I think you do. Look, Jonty, it's time you stopped holding back. It should be blatantly obvious to you now that we suspect Seth Conway of being involved in Leanne's death, at the very least. I've given you my word that your brother will be safeguarded, but so far you've given me little reason to believe that he's in need of protection." Neal leaned forward and pushed his face close to Jonty's. "What are you not telling us, son?"

Ava feared that Jonty would clam up, or demand legal representation, but instead he seemed to be thinking.

"He came up to me one night when I was out with Barney. At Jeffers."

"Jeffers nightclub?" Neal asked.

"Yeah. Lex Thorner was performing some of his songs there that night. Barney loves him, loves musicals. I don't know how Seth knew I was going to be there. He sat down next to me and Barney, and next thing I know he's warning me not to say anything about Leanne and what she'd been up to. He told me to shut up about the past or he'd make sure Barney suffered. And . . . and he asked me about Jess."

"I want to ask you about Jess Stokes now, Jonty," Neal said.

"Is she okay?"

"We don't know. Her landlady hasn't seen her for a couple of days."

"I tried to warn her."

"What do you mean?" Ava was puzzled.

"That day on the bridge . . . I saw her watching. We spoke about Leanne, and Jess told me she knew her when she was at school. Then we spoke again at college a couple of times. She said she was going to try to find out what happened to Leanne." A pause. "So I sent her a note."

"A threatening note?"

"Yes. I was only trying to protect her. I didn't want her crossing Seth."

"What did the note say?" Neal asked.

"It said to stop looking into things that didn't concern her, or people she cared about might get hurt. Something like that. I'm not very good with words. I put it that way because I knew she was a kind person and cared about other people more than herself. I knew that if I threatened her personally she'd just carry on."

Ava leaned back and folded her arms. So much for caring Jonty.

"Did you act on the note?" Neal said.

"What? No! Of course not. I just wanted to put her off. I hated that I had to scare her to do it."

"So you didn't do anything to Jess's neighbour's dog?"

Jonty looked appalled. "You mean hurt it? Hurt a dog? Barney would never forgive me."

Neal pressed on. "Did Jess say anything to you recently? Before her disappearance? Did she tell you that she'd found something significant? Did she know about Seth Conway?"

"No. I don't know." Jonty was becoming agitated. "If he hurts her—"

Neal interrupted. "What do you know about Seth Conway's present whereabouts?"

"Nothing. I don't know where he is, or where Jess could be."

"I don't get it," Ava said. "Jess hadn't seen Leanne for years. Why would Seth see Jess as a threat? Did you tell Seth that Jess was asking questions?"

Jonty shifted in his chair. "No, I swear. I wouldn't put her in danger like that."

"Enough." Neal gave an impatient sweep of his hand. "This interview is terminated." He jabbed at the recorder's off button.

"Are you going to arrest me?" Jonty asked.

"Just . . . go home, son." With a nod to Ava, Neal stood up and strode out of the door.

"So, can I go?" Jonty asked, as if he couldn't believe his luck. Ava gave a shrug. She watched him get up. Sitting down, he had been hunched, deferential. Now, standing at his full height in the confines of the interview room, he was an imposing presence. As if reading her thoughts, he slumped his shoulders and lowered his head.

Ava returned to the office to look for PJ. "Fancy a bite to eat?"

To her surprise, PJ shook her head. "Got weight watchers tonight. I've brought a salad in. Anyway, I think

I'll get to work on tracing that iron, see if I can find the artist."

"Okay, let me know if you need any help."

In need of some fresh air, Ava left the station and walked to the marina. It was a fine day. She considered going for a run, but opted to eat instead. She bought a sandwich and sat on a seat overlooking the river. Something was bothering her. If Jonty hadn't told Seth about Jess's investigations, how come he saw her as a threat? Or even known about her at all? Ava shelved it for now. Questions had a way of finding answers in the long run.

She tore up some bread to throw for the swans and her gaze drifted to the bridge near where Leanne's body had been discovered. Ashley Hunt had said she would likely have died of her wounds if she hadn't drowned. Seth Conway was the kind of monster that Ava would delight in sending down for a very long time. Her appetite gone, Ava shredded what was left of her sandwich and tossed it to the swans. The question of how Seth had found out about Jess still hadn't gone away. It was just on hold.

Back at the station, she found PJ poring over images of narrowboat ware — watering cans and buckets, planters and mugs, brightly decorated in the traditional way with ferns and flowers, roses and castles.

"I never realised how pretty these designs are. Look at the detail on that planter. I might order some of these for my garden."

"Any luck?" Ava asked.

"I've narrowed it down, no pun intended," PJ said. "There's a local woman who runs her own business decorating and selling narrowboat and canal ware. She's also something of an expert on the subject. I was thinking of driving out to see her this afternoon, if that's okay."

"Fine with me. Better just check with the boss. I'm going to make some calls." Ava felt better after her time spent with the swans and she was ready to try skyping Alyssa Ballard.

After eight years in Australia, little of Stromfordshire was left in Alyssa Ballard's accent. "I was really pleased to hear from Leanne," she told Ava. "The timing was perfect. After years of running away from what happened back then, I'd finally made up my mind to speak out. It was such a coincidence hearing from her. As soon as you catch that bastard, I'll book my flight."

Alyssa had attended CAMHS as an adolescent after developing school phobia. She had met Seth there, and attended a number of his 'parties.'

"The thing is," Alyssa said, "I really fancied him. We all did. I didn't want to get him into trouble. He was so good to talk to, you know. I thought he was the only one who really understood what I was going through. Try telling someone you're school phobic — they just laugh. But not Seth. He knew all the right words. I was so naïve."

"You don't need to explain anything to me, Alyssa. You've got nothing to be ashamed of. You were just a child, and Seth took advantage of it."

"How can I help you, Sergeant?"

"I'd like you to concentrate on your conversation with Leanne. Try to remember anything that might help us locate Seth. Did she give you any indication that she knew where he was, or that she'd been in touch with him?"

Alyssa's answer was unexpected.

"She had spoken with him, I know that much. One night she had too much to drink and called him up. She told him she was after him, and he wasn't going to get away with harming any more girls. She was going to make him pay for what he'd done to us. She got his number from someone she worked with, I think. A young girl who knew him when he worked at the Trust and fancied him."

Natalie. Natalie had believed Leanne was seeing Seth. She'd claimed to have overheard a conversation between them, but she'd omitted to mention that it was she who put Leanne in touch with him.

Alyssa's image began to break up on the screen. The connection was going, but it didn't matter. Ava had what she wanted. There was just enough time for her to thank Alyssa before the screen went blank. Ava shut down her laptop with shaky hands.

She burst into Neal's office with the news.

"Good work, Ava," he said. "Contact the Trust and find out if Natalie's there today. If so, get down there and talk to her. PJ can accompany you."

* * *

They pulled up outside the Trust. Ava sighed. "Here we go again. Wouldn't it be just great if people told the truth for once?"

"Don't be too hard on her, Ave. She's just a kid. And she couldn't have known Seth was a killer."

"Hmph." Ava wasn't in the mood for taking prisoners. She did smile at the receptionist, though. She was beginning to regard her as an old friend.

Bryony seemed troubled, concerned for Natalie. "I've asked Natalie to wait in the kitchen," she said. "She's a bit upset. I told her she wasn't in trouble. I hope that was alright?" With a glance at PJ, Ava reassured her that they were just seeking information.

Natalie was red-eyed and frightened. Beth Upton was with her and asked if she could stay.

Ava nodded. "Natalie, I'll come straight to the point. We need to contact Seth Conway as soon as possible. We have reason to believe that he's a very dangerous man. We also know that you gave his contact details to Leanne."

Natalie gave a sob, and held out a pink post-it note.

"This is Seth's number?" Ava asked, incredulous.

Natalie shook her head. "It's the number of the school he was working for after he left here. I don't know his address or anything. I only know that number because

I once overheard him talking to the head of the school just before he left the Trust. I checked his phone when he wasn't looking. I'm sorry I didn't tell you before. I didn't really think about it. I didn't know Seth had done anything wrong. Did . . . did he kill Leanne?"

Ava tried not to show her exasperation. "We don't know. But we do need to question him. It would have helped if you'd thought to give us this information the first time we came."

"Sorry," said Natalie in a shaky voice that made Ava feel like a bully. PJ gave Natalie a sympathetic pat on the shoulder, which only exasperated Ava all the more.

"So you wrote down Seth Conway's number. Were you intending to contact him?"

"I liked him," Natalie said. "I was thinking of contacting him, but then I overheard Bryony telling Beth how he treated that girl at the nightclub. And . . . and then Joe asked me out."

Don't ask, Ava said to herself. "And you gave Seth's contact number to Leanne, why? Did she ask you for it, or did you overhear something she said too?"

Natalie nodded.

"Why on earth did you tell us that you heard Leanne arguing with Seth Conway? Was that even true?"

Natalie hung her head, looking utterly miserable. "I don't know. I just thought—"

"You just thought you'd pay him back for ignoring you by trying to get him involved in a murder investigation?" Ava felt like giving Natalie a good shaking.

Back at the station, Ava called the number Natalie had given her and asked to speak with the principal. It was a school located in Nottinghamshire that specialised in helping children with emotional and behavioural issues.

The principal checked Ava's credentials and called her back. "We had a Seth, but his surname was Richardson, not Conway. He was a visiting mental health nurse who did some therapy sessions with our students."

We had a Seth. Ava's heart soared and sank simultaneously with the principal's use of the past tense. "Does he still do work for the school?"

"No. He was agency. I can send you all the information I have on him and the agency, if that would help."

"Yes, please."

Ava put the phone down.

"He changed his name?" PJ asked.

"It might not be him." They locked eyes. They both knew it was Seth.

"Jesus," said PJ. "Does no one carry out background checks these days? These kids deserve better."

Ava shrugged. "Philippa Patterson couldn't prove Seth assaulted her daughter, and he wasn't sacked from his course, he left voluntarily. He must have continued with his mental health nursing elsewhere, knowing his record was squeaky clean."

Chapter Nineteen

It was nothing like coming round after an anaesthetic. Jess knew about that from the surgery on her back. Now she groped her way back to awareness through a swirling miasma of confusing and frightening dreams. One of these involved being dragged roughly from a car, her head exploding in pain.

The pain in her head was certainly real. Jess groaned and tried to move, but her hands and feet were bound. Where the hell was she? Some light filtered through a dirty skylight on a ceiling low enough to touch. She realised she was lying on a bunk bed in a very small room.

How had she got here?

Jess winced. She attempted to sit up and hit her head on the bunk above. Intense, frightening pain seared through her head and her vision blurred. What if she had concussion and her brain started bleeding?

'I'm alright. Just dizzy,' Jess thought. 'I was at home. Someone was in the pantry. He . . . he hit me.' She tried to conjure up an image of her attacker's face but all she could picture were two pale circles surrounded by blackness. He must have been wearing one of those hats that go right over your head. A balaclava.

Who was the man? Who had brought her here? Jess ran through the men she'd been in contact with recently — Mitch. Henry. Jonty. She went over the events of the past few days. Pam's mugging, the poisoning of Bunty, the warning letter she had found in her letterbox. Mitch had access to her flat. Magda was sometimes careless about who she gave her keys to. Henry had known where Pam lived. It wasn't too much of a leap to suppose he had befriended Pam to get close to her, Jess. And then there was Michael Hollings. He sounded like a nasty piece of work, but why on earth would he want to harm her?

Think, Jess, think. But her head was bursting and her thoughts were all over the place. Then it all began to coalesce.

Leanne.

She had been trying to find out what happened to Leanne. Jess tried to think of all the people who might know about her enquiries. Ava Merry, of course. Pam. Maybe Pam had told Henry. Not Mitch. Who else? Think.

Jonty Cole.

Her mind flashed back to the morning she had stood watching the divers searching the river after Leanne's death. Jonty had been there. He had walked some of the way back to her flat with her. She had told him she knew Leanne. She had even pointed out the road where she lived. Shortly after that, he had started showing an interest in her. She'd thought he fancied her. What if he had more sinister motives? Gingerly, Jess touched her head where the man had struck her. There was a bump and her hair felt sticky. Blood.

It didn't make any sense. Did it? Wait a minute. This man had killed Leanne. Leanne had found out something about him and he had killed her. And now he thought Jess knew. He was going to kill her too.

She began to shake. It was hard to breathe because there was a gag over her mouth. Deep, slow breaths, Jess. You're panicking. You'll hyperventilate if you're not careful. Jess concentrated on her breathing. In, out. In and out. She had to stay calm.

Pam would be missing her. And Mitch. Her colleagues at work. Her parents. They would have raised the alarm. Ava Merry would be looking for her. She was lucky. There were people who cared about her.

It was hard to suppress the dread. What would he do to her when he came back? Jess felt her whole world tip sideways and back, sideways and back. What was happening to her? Was it her head injury? Panic? No, it wasn't her that was moving, it was everything around her. The room was gently swaying to and fro. Bobbing. She was on a boat.

The ropes binding her hands and feet chafed her skin. The gag was too tight, making her retch and the skin around her mouth was raw and bleeding. She lay still, looking up at the sagging underside of the bunk above her and blinked back tears. Every now and then a shudder convulsed her body. Then she heard the sound of tyres crunching on gravel. Her captor was back.

He was still wearing the balaclava. Jess had no idea if it was a good or bad sign that he was hiding his identity. He strode over to where she lay. Jess noticed the plastic carrier wrapped around his hand, and gave a little whimper. Was he intending to suffocate her? Instead he removed her gag, took a water bottle from the bag and unscrewed the cap.

"Who are you?" she asked. "Why have you brought me here?" She wasn't sure she wanted to know the answer to the second question.

He put the bottle to her lips and Jess drank thirstily, choking on the cold water. He took the bottle away and replaced the cap. Jess blinked back tears. It was a good sign that he'd offered her a drink — wasn't it? You don't give water to a person you're about to kill.

"Did you kill Leanne?" Jess asked, suddenly emboldened.

"Shut up," he snapped.

For some reason, even though she knew it would only cause her harm, she began yelling at him, hysterically. "You killed her!"

He slapped her face and she fell silent. He paced up and down for a few minutes, as if in thought. Then, without speaking or even looking at her, he was gone.

Jess lay shaking and exhausted, but she couldn't help feeling a glimmer of hope. She was still alive. He hadn't killed her yet. And that meant there was still time for them to find her.

Chapter Twenty

"How are we getting on with tracing Seth Conway through the nursing agencies?" Neal asked. The agency the principal had mentioned said that Seth Conway — or Richardson as he had been calling himself — had moved on.

PJ looked at her notes. "It's going to be a bit of a long job. There are a fair few nursing agencies that cover Nottinghamshire. I've already been in touch with around six and got contact details for three men called Seth. Only two of them specialise in mental health nursing and only one has been assigned to a post working with children. Seth Carpenter."

"Keep trying," Neal said. He turned to Tom. "Let's go, Tom. Time to interview a couple of unsavoury characters."

It had occurred to Neal that it might be worthwhile tracking down some of their registered paedophiles to see if they remembered Seth or his parties.

"Keep me posted on any leads you or Ava come up with for tracing Seth Conway."

PJ gave a grim smile. "Best eat first. You definitely won't have the stomach for anything later."

* * *

Neal and Tom left the station and made their way to the car park. Things had moved so fast that Neal hadn't had much opportunity to get to know Tom Knight. "Maybe we should take PJ's advice and grab a quick bite to eat," he suggested. They crossed the car park and went into the Duke.

Tom said he didn't miss London, where he'd grown up, although he did miss his family and his friends down south. He had actually attended Stromford University before joining Hertfordshire, and after a couple of years there had decided to relocate to Stromford. He'd liked the city a lot in his student days. Though he seemed willing enough to talk, Neal had the impression that Tom wasn't giving much away.

"So, how are you finding working on my team?" Neal asked.

"All good," Tom replied laconically. "Though since my last DI was Reg Saunders, my bar was set pretty low." Saunders was currently awaiting trial for murder.

"Well, if you put it like that . . . How about Ava? You two getting along?"

"She seems okay. Ambitious. Is she . . . you know . . . in a relationship?"

"Er . . . she was. An A&E doctor at the county, but it didn't last long."

"She's hot."

"Er, yes, she is." They ate in silence for a few moments. Neal suddenly found that he had no appetite, and slid his plate aside.

Tom looked at the chips. "You leaving those?"

"What? Oh yes. Help yourself."

"Don't mind if I do." Tom scooped up the dish.

Neal smiled. "Carry on like that and you'll be putting on weight."

"Nah. Going to the gym later." He grinned and patted his middle.

No doubt he's sporting a six pack under that crisp white shirt, Neal thought, irritably.

He pushed back his chair. "Ready to meet upstanding citizen number one?"

Tom made a face. "As I'll ever be."

Their first destination was roughly twenty minutes' drive away, in a village just south of the city centre.

Neville Burke lived in a terraced council bungalow near the centre of the village, disconcertingly close to a primary school. Most of the bungalows in his row had been fitted with ramps for disabled access. Burke's was one of these.

He looked up at them from a wheelchair. "Whoever you're after, it's not me," he snarled. "I haven't been out the house in weeks."

Neal attempted a sort of smile. "Just a couple of questions if you don't mind, Mr Burke."

Burke led them into his living room. It was small and arranged to accommodate the wheelchair. Burke's laptop sat on a table, lid up, screen blank. Burke had been done in the past for possessing indecent images of young children, as well as grooming offences. It was impossible not to look at that laptop and wonder what he had been looking at before they arrived.

Neal got down to business. He asked if Burke recalled being invited to any parties where Seth had supplied teenage girls for entertainment.

Burke fidgeted with the controls of his wheelchair. Neal had read that he considered himself a reformed man, who'd supposedly found religion and renounced his bad old ways. Somehow it was hard to see him as redeemed. There was something seedy about this room, about Burke's whole demeanour. Tom had placed himself next to the laptop, and from the way Burke kept glancing at it, he had something to hide.

"Name rings a bell," Burke said. "I went to a lot of parties back then." Neal realised that Burke wasn't going to be stupid enough to admit to attending the type of party that might lead him into more trouble with the law.

"Never went to any involving teens myself, but might have heard some rumours at the time."

"What sort of rumours?"

"Mate of a mate, you catch my drift?" Neal nodded. "Said he'd been to a couple of parties where the girls were, er . . . young." Tom moved a little closer to the laptop.

"As in underage?" Neal asked.

"Now that depends on your point of view, doesn't it?"

"No." Tom spoke through gritted teeth. "The law is completely clear on the age of consent."

"Well, if it's the law you're on about."

"Your 'mate,' did he know any of the other men who were there? Did he say where these parties were held?" Neal asked.

Burke looked at his laptop. With a movement of his eyes, Neal signalled for Tom to move away from it. Neal hoped he would understand. Two women were dead, one was missing. Burke was no longer considered a risk to children, given his disability. Whatever sick material was on his laptop, it wasn't their priority right now.

"No to the first question. I . . . I mean . . . he told me the parties took place on a boat. A narrowboat."

Neal and Tom exchanged looks. Both young women had died on a boat, and the murder weapon was a flat iron of the type typically found on a traditional narrowboat.

"Description," Tom snapped.

Burke gave him a sarcastic look. "Well, narrow. .."

"Don't piss us off, Burke." Tom looked at the laptop and Burke shifted in his chair. He gave them a description. For what it was worth after eight years.

"Who owned the boat?" Neal asked. "Was he called Seth?"

Burke shook his head. "He called himself 'the captain.' That's all my friend could tell me." Even if he knew this 'captain's' real name, Burke was unlikely to reveal it.

Neal looked at him. "Does your friend recall what the captain looked like?"

"Well, it was a good eight years ago, but he's probably still on the short side. Bit podgy. Five seven, eight tops. Probably late forties, early fifties. He was pretty grey."

"Anything noteworthy about him?" Neal asked.

Burke rubbed his chin, deliberately making them wait. "He was a bit of a toff."

"What do you mean?" asked Neal. "The way he dressed? How he spoke?"

"Both. Wore one of those stupid silk things round his neck."

"A cravat."

Burke nodded. "And spoke with a plum in his mouth."

It was obvious Burke wasn't going to, or couldn't, name names. Neal asked a few more questions and wrapped up the interview. On their way out, Burke threw them another snippet of information.

"Oh yeah, I just remembered. The captain. He had a funny looking dog. Skinny thing with a shaggy coat?"

Neal waited until they were outside before he spoke. "Henry Bolt." Tom frowned. "Jess Stokes's neighbour Pam struck up a friendship recently with a man called Henry Bolt. He has a borzoi — think hairy greyhound. He's an older man. Met Pam by chance on the common when they were walking their dogs. He could have targeted Pam to get close to Jess, and maybe find out what she knew."

Neal called Ava and instructed her to get round to Pam's place immediately. "If Bolt is there, make sure he doesn't go anywhere, but don't alarm Pam. If he's not there, get his address from Pam and call me back straightaway." He turned to Tom. "Do you know where Millside Road is?" Tom nodded, and Neal told him to get there as quickly as possible — using the siren and a flashing light.

When Neal and Tom arrived, Ava's car was already parked in the reserved parking area outside Jess and Pam's house. "Park behind her," Neal said, hand on the door handle. Outside the house, Tom banged on the front door. Ava opened, shaking her head.

She led them into the hallway. "He's not here. Pam hasn't seen much of him lately."

"Since Jess's disappearance?" Ava nodded. "Does she have his address? A contact number?"

"No."

"Damn it!" If there'd been a wall within punching distance, Neal's fist would have been through it. He glared at Tom, who flinched.

"Has Henry done something wrong?" Pam's voice, thin and fearful, issued from the stairway.

"I'll speak with her," Ava volunteered.

"She'll have to be told," Neal said, grim-faced. "And if she has any idea where Henry might be, we need to know. Fast. I'll be outside in the car." Neal turned around, stumbling against Tom who had been hovering in the doorway. Neal jerked a thumb at the car, and Tom pressed the key fob to unlock the doors.

Tom seated himself at the wheel. "Now what?"

Neal gave no answer.

* * *

"I should have known. He was just too good to be true." Pam sighed. "But never mind that, what about Jess? If Henry is capable of killing an innocent dog, who knows what else he might be capable of!"

Ava asked Pam to think hard about where she thought Henry might be, or how they could find out. Pam sat pummelling her cheeks with her fist until Ava worried that she might hurt herself. She waited by the window, gazing down at the street, and saw a traffic warden approach the car where Neal and Tom Knight were parked. When she saw the passenger-side window wind down and the poor warden lean in, Ava cringed and turned away.

"Of course! Boris." Pam leapt up.

"The dog?"

"Henry's dog. He's ten years old. No dog gets to that age without a few health problems. My Bunty—"

Ava cut her off. "Thanks, Pam. I'll get someone on to checking out the vets' surgeries straightaway."

"No, no, you don't have to. I know where Henry took Boris."

Ava jotted down the name and address and promised to let her know if there was any news about Jess. She didn't have the heart to tell Pam that they might already be too late.

Neal's window was still rolled down, and the traffic warden retreating, when Ava leaned in on Tom's side of the car. "I've got a lead. PJ's getting in touch with the vet on Blackberry Lane. She's going to call straight back." Ava slid into the back seat. "Henry's dog, Boris, is registered there. Pam thinks they'll have Henry's address."

Ava's phone soon rang, and she put PJ on speaker.

"Bloody hell, Ava, I thought they were going to demand a flipping warrant."

Tom drove off before PJ had finished reading the address. Neal punched the postcode into the Satnav. Ava had no choice but to go along too, and leave her own car at the mercy of the next traffic warden.

* * *

Henry Bolt was in his front garden halfway up a stepladder, watering a hanging basket outside his front door. The watering can was green, with a floral design of red, white and pink roses, a splendid example of canal art.

"Nice watering can," Ava said, and opened the garden gate. Neal and Tom were a formidable presence right behind her.

Henry didn't even blink. "Good afternoon. Yes, it is rather pretty, isn't it? 'Have nothing in your house that you do not know to be useful, or believe to be beautiful . . .' Personally, I believe that even useful things should be beautiful — or at least not ugly."

The water ran to a trickle, and then stopped altogether. "Excuse me while I refill my can." Henry climbed down from the ladder and stepped back to admire the basket, full of cascading petunias and trailing lobelias, and dripping water around Henry's feet.

"I don't think so." Ava reached for the watering can and prised it from his grasp. She proceeded to caution him and informed him that he would be accompanying them back to the station for questioning. Even that didn't wipe the genial smirk off his face.

"At least let me arrange for someone to take care of Boris." Hearing his name, the dog appeared in the doorway, wagging its tail uncertainly. He was wearing one of those knotted check ties around his neck instead of a collar and looked as dapper as his owner.

"Like you took care of Pam's Bunty," Ava said, giving Boris an apologetic look.

Henry gave an exaggerated shudder. "Don't mention that ugly bitch in my presence — the dog, I mean."

"Where is Jess Stokes?" Ava asked.

"I couldn't say, my dear."

"Take him to the car," Neal instructed Tom. He took Boris by the scarf and led him inside the house. Ava followed and closed the door behind them. Everything about the décor in Henry Bolt's house was tasteful and bespoke. The kitchen had freestanding units which had been painted in shades of duck egg, cream and sky blue. A huge dresser stood against one wall, displaying an assortment of canal ware — jugs and bowls, spoons, plates, cups and teapots. Canal ware planters overflowing with fragrant herbs stood all along the window sill.

"He really likes this stuff," Ava remarked. Boris sidled up to her and licked her hand. She gazed down at him, wondering how much he would miss his master if Henry proved to be the mysterious 'captain' they were looking for.

Jess wasn't in the house. They pulled out furniture to look for hidden spaces and checked the loft and the garage but there was no evidence to suggest that she had ever been there. "We'll rip the place apart," Neal said, "Just in case."

They joined Tom outside. He was standing by the car with Henry, who seemed to be taking this more seriously now. They drove back to the station, with Ava sitting beside Henry and Boris lying across their feet, blissfully unaware of what was taking place.

They walked into the station.

"I want a lawyer," Henry said, predictably. Neal looked at his watch, wearily. He nodded at Ava and she went to make the call. They were promised someone within the hour. It was going to be a long night.

PJ was eager to tell them what she'd found. "I spoke with that woman who sells canal ware. She recognised the design I sent her and confirmed that she'd sold two flat irons like that about six months ago. She only did a limited number in that design and she still had the order details on file. The customer said he was planning to use them as bookends. His name was Henry Bolt. And I thought *I'd* made a breakthrough."

"You did, Peej, the DI and Tom just got a lucky break. What you've got is sound evidence."

"Did you get a chance to search Bolt's place? Did you find another iron?" PJ asked.

"Yes, we searched it." Ava tried to picture the canal ware on the dresser in Bolt's kitchen. "No, I'm sure there wasn't an iron."

"Must be on his boat then," PJ said. Their eyes met. Ava knew they were both thinking the same thing. Jess could be on Bolt's boat.

If she was still alive.

Chapter Twenty-One

Much to Ava's distaste, Henry's legal representative was Liz Marlborough, who had defended the woman who had stabbed Neal's sister the previous year. Not an auspicious start. She watched Neal acknowledge Marlborough with a brief nod, and felt for him.

Were they looking at Leanne's killer? Ava wondered. Neville Burke had been shown Henry's picture, had verified that Henry was the man he'd seen at the parties years ago and had known as the 'captain.' It might be enough to take to the CPS to request permission to make a formal charge. Time was of the essence. They couldn't hold Henry indefinitely without one. If Henry had information that might lead them to Jess, they needed to get him to talk. Fast.

The present interview was intended to establish Henry's involvement in what appeared to be a case of historical abuse, and to find out what he knew about Seth Conway and his possible abduction of Jess Stokes.

Neal shot through the preliminaries, and the interview began.

"Mr Bolt," he said. "We have a witness who has confirmed that you were present when the sexual abuse of underage girls took place on your narrowboat on a number of occasions between May and July, 2006. What do you have to say about this?" Henry looked to Liz Marlborough.

She said, "My client has expressed his wish to cooperate fully with your investigation."

Ava was suddenly hopeful. Had Henry been advised that admitting his guilt might mitigate his likely sentence? She wondered what Henry had told Marlborough to elicit such advice.

"Yes," Henry said.

"You admit to being present on all of the occasions when the alleged abuse took place?" Neal asked.

"Yes."

"You were the owner of the narrowboat where the offences took place?"

"Yes."

"Mr Bolt, were you actively engaged in the sexual abuse of a number of underage girls eight years ago?" Henry gave another glance at Liz Marlborough, who nodded.

"Y . . . yes." The room seemed to chill a few degrees. "B . . . but they were—"

Neal raised a warning hand. "No excuses. I don't want to hear that these girls were willing participants. They were children."

"It was just sex," Henry muttered.

"Excuse me?"

Henry repeated his statement.

Ava struggled to suppress her revulsion. Just sex. What was 'just sex' to Henry Bolt had resulted in at least four deaths that they knew of. How many other young lives had been destroyed by the evil actions of these men? Earlier in the day, Ava had seen the lab report on the DNA extracted from Ruby Kennedy's fingernails. Would it be a match for Henry's? Henry Bolt was a lot of things

— perverted and morally skewed, cowardly and self-deluded — but was he also a killer?

Child abuse had touched Ava's own life. Her best friend at university had committed suicide following years of abuse. Ava had subsequently dropped out. It was one of the reasons she found cases involving sexual abuse so hard to bear. But then crimes involving children were hard for everyone to cope with.

Neal leaned back and gave Ava a nod.

"Did you kill Leanne Jackson?" she asked.

"No."

"Did you kill Ruby Kennedy?"

"No."

"What do you know about the disappearance of Jess Stokes?"

Silence. For the record, Ava said, "Mr Bolt has chosen not to answer."

Henry changed his mind. "I don't know anything about that."

Ava leaned forward across the table. "I think you do."

"It's the truth."

"Tell us about your relationship with Seth Conway."

"I don't have a relationship with Seth Conway."

"Mr Bolt. Two women are dead, and another has been abducted. The weapon used to kill Leanne Jackson was a flat iron. It was one of a pair intended for use as bookends. The artist who painted her unique design on both irons has confirmed that she sold these items to you in January this year. We have copies of the receipts, and the artist has also identified you from pictures shown to her by our officers. All of this leads us to suspect that you played some part in the murder of Leanne Jackson. If your DNA or fingerprints are on the iron you could be facing a murder charge."

The interview room was so cool that Ava had goose bumps on her forearms, but Henry had broken out in a sweat. He was afraid. It showed in his nervous movements, in the damp patches under his arms and in his restless eyes darting around the room, seeking out everything but Neal's hard stare. Sitting beside him, Marlborough, crisp and cool in her navy linen shift dress, gave him a slight nod.

"I swear I don't have anything to do with the deaths of those women. Seth contacted me a few weeks ago. He told me Leanne Jackson was onto us. She'd been following up on former clients of that Trust she worked for and started putting two and two together. She remembered a couple of names from her time at CAHMS and started looking up other girls who went to CAHMS at the same time. That's how she met up with Ruby Kennedy. She was trying to persuade Ruby to go to the police, tell them about the parties. Testify." Henry spat this last word out as if it burnt his mouth. "Seth came to tell me the game was up. The Jackson girl was like a terrier with a rat — she'd never let go and she'd almost certainly persuade those girls to cry historical abuse. Seth was planning on going abroad. He'd already changed his identity at least once already, in order to carry on working in this country. I was making plans along those lines too, when all of a sudden Jackson and her friend turned up dead."

Ava glanced at Marlborough. She gave a shrug as if to say that's what she'd been told too. But Henry knew more. Everyone in the room was sure of it.

"So what are you saying now, Henry? That Leanne Jackson and Ruby Kennedy were murdered by some mystery third party totally unrelated to their sexual abuse? That even though we have evidence that links both you and Seth with the two murdered women, the pair of you aren't involved in any way?" Neal's voice mingled disbelief with contempt.

"Tell us about your relationship with Pam Hollings. You didn't meet her by chance while walking your dog, did you?"

A look of revulsion flickered across Henry's face. "No. That wasn't my idea. I wouldn't have gone within a mile of that cow and her mongrel."

"So whose idea was it? Seth's?" Neal asked. A flicker of something else besides fear crossed Henry's face. His next words couldn't have been more unexpected.

"I have a kid." Liz Marlborough looked at him in surprise. "A daughter. She lives with her mother." He gave a thin laugh. "For obvious reasons. But that doesn't mean I don't love her. I want to know that she'll be protected." It was like listening to Jonty Cole all over again. Seth had threatened Henry in the same way that he had threatened Jonty — by going after the person he loved.

"Seth threatened to harm your daughter if you spoke to us?" Neal asked.

There was a silence. Henry stared down at his hands. Then he glanced nervously at Marlborough, who was now giving him clear signals to shut up. Ava was expecting her to intervene, request a break so that she could find out what the hell Henry hadn't told her. But he was unstoppable.

"Not Seth," he said at last. For a second there was absolute silence. No one breathed.

"Who?" Neal asked. "Mystery man?"

"He's got my boat," Henry said petulantly.

Neal's patience was at an end. "Who?"

Henry's voice dropped to a whisper. "The first time he came to one of my parties he was rough with one of the girls. More than rough. He beat her half to death. Seth had to pull him off. I didn't stand for that sort of thing. I ordered him off my boat." His voice dropped to a whisper. "The man you're looking for is called Jonty Cole. He's a monster."

Ava let out a gasp.

Neal's fist slammed down so hard on the recorder stop control that the whole table shook. He declared the interview over and stood up abruptly, his chair tipping away behind him and landing with a crash on the floor. It was left to Ava to conclude the proceedings and wait while Henry was conveyed to a holding cell.

She kept thinking, *Fuck. We had the bastard and we let him walk. We let him walk.*

She sought Neal out immediately. He had already set the wheels in motion. Every police officer in Stromford would now be on the lookout for Jonty Cole. Ava thought of Henry's look of distaste when he mentioned the girl Jonty had beaten half to death. *Oh, Jess,* she thought, knowing they might be too late to find her alive.

Chapter Twenty-two

Jonty checked the locks twice before leaving the boat. The last thing he wanted was for some prowler to break into the boat and spoil everything. Jess's bindings were securely tied, and there was no way she'd be able to work them loose.

He drove up the muddy track to the nearest road, casting a look back at the narrowboat in its mooring. Was he doing the right thing leaving it hiding almost in plain sight? He could easily have taken to the waterways and been miles away by now. If it hadn't been for Barney, he probably would have cruised off right after that interview.

That detective had taken him by surprise accosting him in the college car park like that. He shouldn't have run. It was the kind of stupid thing Seth would have done. Thinking with his feet instead of his head.

It was over, he knew. The police were all over Seth for Leanne and Ruby's murders, but as soon as they tracked him down, they'd learn the truth. Jonty hoped he'd bought himself enough time. If not, he still had the Stokes bitch as a bargaining chip. Shame. He'd been looking forward to beating her slowly to death.

Jonty knew he was taking a risk in going back for Barney. If the police were onto him they'd be round at Barney's place like a shot. But he was confident he'd managed to convince them that Seth was the villain they were after. They'd be looking elsewhere for a bit. Still, he needed to act without delay.

Chapter Twenty-three

No one was surprised that Jonty Cole had gone to ground.

By the time they arrived to conduct a search of the furnished flat he had been renting on Stromford Road, he'd cleared it of all his personal belongings.

"He hasn't lived here in days," said Neal. "He's been hiding out on Bolt's boat."

Henry Bolt had given them a description of his narrowboat, but Jonty would certainly have disguised and renamed it since he took up residence. CCTV footage of the stretch of river leading to the marina from the night Leanne and Ruby died had revealed that a narrowboat had passed under the bridge about half an hour before Leanne's body was discovered. The trouble was, in the darkness there was nothing to see but a long shadow, black and anonymous. A search of the canals and rivers was already underway, but the River Strom was connected to a whole network of waterways and by now Jonty could be almost anywhere.

"We know he's been in touch with Seth recently. If Bolt was telling the truth, Jonty must have been blackmailing Seth," Neal said.

Ava nodded. "Seth must have panicked, told Jonty that Leanne was onto him and he was going abroad, so Jonty decided to deal with the problem." She sighed and pulled off her latex gloves.

"Let's go," said Neal. "Your mate Dan will be here shortly. There's no need for us to linger."

They left a uniformed officer at the door and made their way back to the station.

PJ told them that her trawl of the nursing agencies in Nottingham had narrowed to two men, either of whom might be Seth Conway. She grinned. "That's the good news."

Neal's mood was as stormy as a Hebridean island in winter. "Just give me the facts, Constable."

"Sorry, sir. One of them was registered under a bogus address, and the other has moved to Scotland. The one who moved to Scotland is a fifty-two-year-old Polish man, so he's unlikely to be our Seth."

Ava gave PJ a pat on the shoulder. "Nice try, Peej."

Neal stormed into his office. He soon felt ashamed. It wasn't PJ's fault the trail had gone cold. Neal had been so sure that tracing Seth Conway would lead them closer to Jess Stokes. Now, with every hour that passed, the likelihood of finding her alive was more remote.

Neal stared at his screen, poring over the case notes. Something was niggling him. Why had Jonty attended CAMHS? He'd never really told them. Neal recalled something that Tina Jackson had said about Leanne being in a relationship with an abusive boyfriend she'd met at CAMHS. The boyfriend had been attending anger management sessions. It was a bit of a leap, but what if the boyfriend had been Jonty Cole? He'd attended CAMHS at the same time as Leanne and the others. Even if Leanne had not been lured to any of Seth and Henry's boat parties, she must have known that Jonty was involved. What else had she discovered about Jonty Cole?

Neal called Tom Knight into his office and asked him to send a PC back to Tina Jackson's to show her some pictures of Jonty, then and now. Then he called Ava, PJ and Tom into his room. They had been working this case for nearly ten days now and the strain was beginning to tell. He knew he was showing it too — Jock had commented on it the previous evening.

Neal was also feeling guilty about seeing so little of his son, Archie. In the past couple of weeks, Jock had been taking Archie out with Maggie, and Archie was having a great time. Lying awake in the early hours of the morning, Neal wondered what he would do if Maggie returned to Scotland with Jock. Archie wasn't a little kid any more. At the end of the summer he'd be starting secondary school, but Neal wanted to be there for him. He sighed. What was he doing, thinking about this now with three expectant faces all looking at him in anticipation?

"Let's take a minute to consider where we are with this case. We know how our two main suspects connect to the girls on Leanne's list, and to Leanne herself. We know that Seth Conway recruited sixteen-year-old Jonty Cole to help him entice the girls he met at CAMHS to his boat parties, and from what Henry Bolt told us about Cole's behaviour towards one of the girls, Cole has a violent temper. Let's consider that Jonty Cole might have been the violent ex-boyfriend of Leanne's that Tina Jackson alluded to when you interviewed her."

Neal looked at PJ and Tom. "Hence my request that you send someone out to show Tina some pictures." He looked at his team, seeing weariness but also a determination to see the case through. "If we had the resources, I'd have men and women out there searching every narrowboat in the county and beyond, but we know that's not possible. So if anyone has any ideas? I hate to use the old cliché, but we really do need to think outside the box."

"Barney," Ava said immediately. "Jonty's brother. We know that Jonty is devoted to him. Would he just abandon him, do you think?"

"We've already had a couple of officers out to search the assisted living facility where Barney lives. The staff there know to contact us immediately if Jonty shows up."

"Jess was fond of Barney. I wonder if that worked both ways."

"What are you thinking, Ava?" Neal asked.

"That perhaps Jonty kidnapped Jess for reasons that are completely unconnected with the rest of this case."

"You mean Barney was in love with her?" PJ said.

Ava nodded. "What if Jonty kidnapped Jess not because he was afraid Leanne had been in touch with her, but because he had feelings for her?" Ava's face lit up. "If that is the case, it makes it much more likely that Jess could still be alive."

Neal wondered if Ava was clutching at straws, but it didn't feel like it. It was way out of the box, but wasn't that exactly what he'd asked for?

"We need to speak with CAMHS again, this time about Jonty Cole. It would be useful to have a professional's input on the kind of mind we're dealing with here."

"Sir," Ava said. "I'd like permission to stay over at Barney's place. If I'm right, Jonty's taken Jess because he sees the three of them — himself, Jess and Barney — as a neat little family unit. He'll come back for his brother. I can talk to Barney too. He might reveal something helpful if I gain his trust."

Neal deliberated. He was extremely reluctant to put his officers at risk. Particularly Ava, who had demonstrated in the past that she was prepared to cross a line if she thought it might get a result. He looked at her face. It was so full of hope for Jess that he didn't really have a choice.

"Alright," he agreed at last. "But you take no unnecessary risks. Is that understood?"

"Absolutely, sir," replied Ava.

"Let's set it up," Neal said. "Tom, contact that psychologist and get me a report on Jonty Cole."

Chapter Twenty-four

Jess lay still. If it hadn't been for the throbbing pain in her head, she might actually have dozed off, soothed by the boat's rhythmic bobbing. Like the flow of a tidal river, her fear rose and fell. The sound of a car departing shortly after he left her caused an ebb, but with every hour that passed, a tsunami threatened.

Jess thought of Leanne, sinking into the Strom, her final choking gasps as water replaced the remaining air in her lungs. It didn't matter how good a swimmer you were. Even a strong swimmer like Ava Merry would succumb eventually. She'd read once that in the past, sailors preferred not to learn to swim. Better to go quickly than struggle against the inevitable. How long did it take to drown? Minutes?

Despite her fear, Jess was angry. Who the hell did this man think he was, kidnapping her, tying her up and leaving her alone in the darkness with a head wound that might prove fatal?

What would Ava Merry do in a situation like this? she wondered. She certainly wouldn't lie around feeling sorry for herself.

Jess twisted around on the mattress. The springs creaked and pinged. She felt around, seeking a tear in the fabric. After minutes of tortuous wriggling and shifting, her fingers slipped through a slit in the fabric and touched cold metal. Her heart leapt. She wrapped her fingers around a tuft of material and pulled.

Fortunately it was a cheap mattress, inadequately padded. Ignoring her breaking nails, Jess ripped at the cloth until she could slip her fingers through and search for a sharp edge. At last she felt something jab her wrist and she began to saw her wrist ties backwards and forwards, until she felt them begin to loosen. After what seemed hours of yanking and pulling, Jess was rubbing her chafed and bleeding wrists. She tore off the gag, and then turned to her feet. In the dim light she had to grope and feel for the knots. Then she was free.

She rubbed hard at her numb legs, and pushed up onto her knees. Like a fern, she uncurled slowly until she was upright.

She swayed on her feet for a moment, fighting back nausea and dizziness, and then groped her way to the door. It was locked. Of course. But how sturdy could a door on a narrowboat be? Jess drew back one leg ready to kick. And froze, her leg in mid-air. The sound of a car engine was growing louder and closer. She stood like that for a moment, and then made up her mind. Whatever happened next, she would be better equipped to deal with it out of this confined space and in the light. She drove her foot hard against the door and it crumpled at once.

There was no sudden dazzle of daylight. Jess had an impression of a long, narrow living space, curtained and dark. She crossed to a window and moved the curtain aside. The towpath was tantalisingly close but the car was already pulling up. There would be no time to get off the boat unseen. Jess looked around for a place to hide, something to use as a weapon.

Her gaze fell on a block of kitchen knives and she grabbed the one with the largest handle. A bread knife. No good. The second largest had a serrated edge and a sharp, pointed blade. Perfect. Armed with the knife, Jess positioned herself behind a flimsy partition and waited.

The boat listed to one side when the man stepped on board.

She heard him shuffle, moving forward cautiously. Now he was in the room with her. She had an unbearable urge to peek around the partition. Was this even the same man? The thought struck her suddenly, and her heart soared.

He wasn't Mitch.

She flattened herself against the partition and tightened her grip on the knife. He was close now, so close that Jess could hear him breathe. He stepped into view. Jess tensed, expecting him to sense her presence, spin around. But he walked right past the partition. His back was to her now. Leanne's face flashed into her mind. She would never have a better chance.

Chapter Twenty-five

The supervisor, an Eastern European woman called Mariana, introduced Ava to the staff as, one by one, they arrived for their afternoon shift. She showed Ava around the assisted living facility, starting with the communal area, where residents could meet to socialise or prepare a snack. Only two residents were there, because, Mariana explained, most of the others worked or attended activities throughout the day. The communal area was open plan. Facing the entrance was a reception desk, where visitors had to report to gain access to the rest of the building.

"They have to buzz to get into the building in the first place," Mariana explained, pointing to the controlled entry door. She had seemed shocked when the police had turned up asking about Jonty Cole and insisting on searching his brother's flat. Now that Ava had given her a little more information, Mariana seemed keen to help.

"I steel cannot believe," she said. "Jonty seem like such lovely person. We all love him here. Many of our residents, they never have visitors. Families stick them here and forget about them. Not so Jonty Cole. So devoted to his brother. Last night, first time he let Barney down. He was supposed to take Barney bowling. I didn't know what to tell Barney when Jonty not turn up."

"It's important that we don't let Barney suspect anything," Ava said. "We don't want to alarm him. And we don't want him to give anything away to Jonty if he turns up."

"Of course," promised Mariana. She gave Ava a set of keys to Barney's flat, and to an empty flat next door where she would be able to work. Neal had arranged a video conference to discuss what they had learned from the psychologist who had worked with Jonty Cole eight years ago.

Barney's flat was on the first floor. An L-shaped hallway led in one direction to a living room and kitchen area, in the other to a bedroom, and straight ahead to a bathroom.

The walls of Barney's bedroom were decorated with posters of his favourite football team, Manchester United. There was a picture of Jonty on his bedside table. The clothes in his wardrobe were arranged according to colour. The main living area had a wide flat-screen TV on the wall which, Mariana explained, had been installed by Jonty so that he and Barney could watch football and movies together. Barney also had a big collection of DVDs, mostly action movies. Ava's eyes were drawn to a framed photograph of Barney and Jess on the windowsill. Barney was holding up a certificate. Presumably Jonty had taken the picture.

Ava left Barney's flat and let herself in next door. The flat was completely empty. She installed herself on the floor and took out her laptop ready for the meeting. The reception wasn't brilliant but Ava could see all three of her colleagues, three giant heads filling the screen.

"Hi, Ava!" PJ gave her a wave and Ava grinned back. Neal was looking stern and Tom was looking down, presumably at his notes.

"Hello, Ava," Neal began. "Tom and PJ have had an interesting meeting with Dr Tobias Warren at CAMHS. I'll let Tom fill you in."

Tom looked up. "Hi, Ava. So, Dr Warren remembered Jonty Cole. He'd read over his case notes before seeing us, although he did say that he would have remembered Cole in any case," Tom paused, "because he was 'such an intriguing personality,' as the good doctor put it."

Like all the best psychos, Ava thought.

Tom continued, "Jonty was referred to CAMHS after a particularly nasty incident involving two girls from his school. He basically laid into them right in the middle of the High Street after they called him and his brother names. He had to be dragged off them. Both required hospital treatment."

"Barney witnessed the assault?"

Tom nodded. "Yeah. Actually, Barney got upset and had to be restrained by a couple of CSOs."

"What about criminal proceedings?" Ava asked. "Jonty must have been, what, fifteen, nearly sixteen?"

"The girls didn't press charges. Apparently they were notorious bullies. Jonty claimed he'd gone into meltdown because they'd targeted his disabled brother. He managed to convince everyone it was a one off, and that he was being protective. Dr Warren said that sometimes kids with a disabled sibling bottle up their emotions. They can feel anger and resentment, but feel guilty if they show it. Barney was pushed onto Jonty from a young age. Their dad made himself scarce as soon as it became apparent that Barney had problems. His mum self-medicated for a while before being diagnosed with depression. You have to hand it to Jonty, he all but brought his kid brother up single-handedly." Tom's face was grim. "But before you start feeling all warm and cuddly towards him, listen to this. The good doctor wasn't convinced."

"By what?" Ava asked.

Tom looked at her. "By any of it."

"Meaning?"

"Meaning he thought Jonty was using Barney as a cover for his psychopathy." So much for my brilliant idea, thought Ava. If Jonty Cole was a psychopath, her theory about him having feelings for Jess was wrong. He wouldn't be capable of feelings.

"Even so, Warren found Jonty's relationship with his brother intriguing and puzzling. Warren pointed out he wasn't an expert on psychopaths — he's a clinical psychologist who specialises in child and adolescent mental health. So he discussed Jonty with a psychiatrist colleague, who thought that Jonty acted as he did towards his brother because he'd seen that other people thought well of him for it. Barney was useful to him. He showed Jonty in a good light, and Jonty liked the image of himself as the sainted brother. In time, that image would have become part of his identity. Barney was necessary to him, as well as useful."

"So what are we dealing with? A psychopath, or not?" Ava asked.

Neal answered. "Warren was cagey about giving a precise diagnosis. Narcissistic personality disorder, psychopath, it doesn't really matter now that we know what Jonty's capable of. The professionals can argue over it later. Proceed with extreme caution, Ava. If Jonty does turn up, call for backup immediately."

"Yes, sir." Ava closed down her laptop. This profile of Jonty Cole gave her little reason to hope that Jess was still alive. She paced the empty flat. Mariana had assured her that Barney would be back soon. College was closing early for some kind of training session and he was due any time. Ava was still pacing when a taxi pulled up. She crossed to the window and peered through the net curtains. Barney was making his way towards the entrance.

Ava took the stairs three at a time and was waiting in the communal area when Barney walked in. Mariana appeared from nowhere, and Barney gave her a hug. Then he caught sight of Ava. He pulled away from Mariana and rushed over to embrace her.

Mariana followed him over and said, “Ava would like to have a chat with you, Barney. Is ok with you?” Barney nodded enthusiastically.

“How about right here? I’ll bring us some drinks?”

“Hot chocolate for me,” Barney said immediately.

“I know, I know, Barney. Coffee for you, Sergeant Merry?”

Barney led her to a seating area with sofas and chairs arranged around a huge TV screen.

“Movie night tonight,” Barney told her in his hesitant, childlike voice. “Me choose.”

“What are you going to watch, Barney?” Ava asked. Barney pulled a DVD off a bookshelf and showed her.

“Harry Potter and the Prisoner of Azkaban. Hey, good choice. That’s one of my favourites.” Barney’s face lit up.

Ava risked a question. “How is that brother of yours, Barney? Jonty, isn’t it?”

Barney looked crestfallen. “Missed bowling last night.”

“Oh, that’s a shame. I’m sure Jonty had a good reason for missing it.”

“Yes. Good reason.” His disappointment was so palpable it caused Ava to contemplate for the first time just how devastating losing his brother would be. If he was guilty of murdering at least two women, Jonty faced a life sentence. Just like that, poor Barney’s life would fall apart.

“Barney, does your brother have a boat?”

“No.”

“Has he ever taken you on a boat? One of those long ones that you see on the river in town sometimes?”

Barney’s face lit up. “Yes. In town. Hot chocolate and cakes.”

"He means the one that's moored near Marks and Spencer," Mariana said. She set down a tray of drinks on the table in front of them. "Jonty takes you there on Saturdays sometimes, doesn't he, Barney?"

Ava knew it. She'd often passed the floating café, but had never gone inside.

"What's that you've got there, Barney?" Mariana picked up the DVD and turned it over. "Oh, Harry Potter. We are watching that later?"

Ava smiled at Barney's enthusiastic nodding. "That's a new one," Mariana said. "Barney watch old one so often, he wear it out."

"Who's your favourite character?" Ava asked.

Barney beamed. "'Mione. Pretty."

"Hey, mine too," Ava said. They high-fived.

An idea struck her. "Excuse me a sec," she said. She pulled her phone out and called Neal. In a low voice, she said, "It's just a hunch, sir, but there's a possibility Jonty might have named his boat the 'Hermione' to please his brother. Harry Potter's his favourite film and he's sweet on Hermione. Not much, I know, but it might help with the search."

"Barney would like to show you his room," Mariana said.

She left them at the door.

Barney beckoned Ava inside. She gazed around, pretending she was seeing everything for the first time.

Chapter Twenty-six

"Call for you." Tom Knight handed PJ the phone. She looked at him but he shook his head. The caller hadn't given a name.

"Detective Constable Polly Jenkins speaking." No response. "Hello?" Was Tom playing silly buggers?

PJ heard a sigh. "My name is Andrea," said the caller.

"Andrea? How can I help you?"

"I'm a care support assistant in Nottingham. I work for an agency called Star Healthcare."

PJ recognised the name from her enquiries about Seth. "Go on."

"I think you were making enquiries about Seth Carpenter?"

"That's right, Andrea. Do you have some information for me?"

"I think I know where you can find him." PJ held her breath. "I don't know why you're interested in Seth, but I can make a pretty good guess. He's into young girls. Am I right?"

"You're sort of in the right ballpark," PJ said. "What else do you know?" Another silence. Terrified that the caller was going to hang up, PJ managed to keep her voice steady. "Andrea, I'm not exaggerating when I say that a woman's life might depend on what you say next."

Tom Knight had moved closer and PJ put the call on speaker.

"I can't prove anything."

"That's okay. Just tell me what you believe."

"Seth doesn't work for the agency now, as you were probably told. I heard our manager telling you that he'd given you a false address. While he was here he got a job at a mental health charity called Think Ahead. They provide advice and support for teenagers with mental health problems. They do a lot of outreach work. Visit kids in their homes and work with their families. I'm assuming you get what the attraction of this kind of work would be for someone like Seth?"

PJ had a sinking feeling. "Yes, all too well." Beside her, Tom signalled for the receiver.

"Andrea, this is Detective Sergeant Tom Knight speaking. In a minute, we'd be really grateful if you'd allow us to pass you onto a colleague of ours to make a statement. But right now, what we need from you is information on where to find Seth Calder. As DC Jenkins just said, a woman's life might depend on it."

"Okay, you can hear my story later. Have you got a pen ready?" Andrea read out an address and PJ scribbled it down.

"So, he's back in Stromfordshire," PJ said to Tom, surprised. "Brantalby. There's a train station there. He could move easily between Stromford and Nottingham.

"I know it," Tom said. "Better tell the chief."

PJ tapped on Neal's window. He beckoned them in and listened to what PJ had to say.

"You've checked this Andrea out?" he asked. "She is who she claims to be?"

"Er . . ."

"I'm on it," Tom said. His thumbs darted rapidly across the screen of his phone. PJ was furious at herself for making such a rookie error, but at least she wasn't alone. Tom had too. She twisted a strand of hair nervously around her finger and waited.

"She checks out," Tom said. "The agency confirmed that they have an Andrea Barber on their books."

But Neal's mobile was ringing. PJ noticed a vein throbbing at his temple. Exhaustion? Or worry?

"Yes, yes. Please check his room immediately." Neal's voice bristled with impatience. He lowered the phone.

PJ risked the question. "Is everything alright, sir?"

"The manager at Barney Cole's place said that a member of staff saw Jonty leave with Barney about ten minutes ago. Apparently Barney looked upset. She didn't see Ava." They waited, rigid with suspense, for the manager to call back. The phone rang.

Something's wrong. PJ saw it immediately in Neal's expression.

"Have you called 999?" he rasped. "Why the hell not? Call right now. I'm on my way!"

Come on. PJ wanted to shake Neal. It had to be Ava who needed the paramedics, right? Neal was raking his hand through his hair.

"DI Knight, DC Jenkins, I want you to go to Seth Conway's address. If he's there, arrest the bastard."

"Hang on a minute! What's going on? Is Ava okay? What's happened?" PJ's words tumbled out, all formalities forgotten.

"The manager found her on the bathroom floor in Barney's flat. She's unconscious. That's all I know," Neal said. He looked at PJ and added, "As soon as there's any news, I'll call you."

PJ held her DI's gaze for as long as she dared, hoping he would understand that she loved Ava too.

* * *

Not since his ex-partner Myrna had announced that she was in labour had Neal felt such a compulsion to be somewhere before he'd even set out. He'd experienced a moment of blind panic when Mariana described how she'd found Ava lying unconscious on the floor of Barney Cole's bathroom. At least she'd had the sense to check that Ava had a pulse before calling him back. He couldn't believe that her first instinct hadn't been to call an ambulance.

The way PJ's eyes had bored into his. She knows. Was it so obvious then, this feeling he had for Ava that he wouldn't acknowledge, even to himself? To think he was brazen enough to chide Jock over his feelings for Maggie! Neal was a deeply private man. PJ's look had made him feel terribly vulnerable.

His phone rang again, and he heard the manager's voice.

"The ambulance is here. DS Merry has regained consciousness. She asked me to give you a message. It's a bit weird — I think she might be concussed. But she was very insistent."

"Go on," Neal said.

"She said to tell you Hermione's moored at the haunted tower. Barney was talking about watching Harry Potter earlier and Hermione's his favourite character. Maybe—"

Neal ended the call.

Ava had regained consciousness. Was that a good sign? Neal's gut churned. What to do? He could send a patrol car to the Hermione, leave it to others to bring Ava's attacker in. Or, he could stick a blue light on his car and race to the hospital.

Neal steeled himself, and grabbed his car keys. This was what Ava wanted, wasn't it? She'd left the message for him because she wanted him to catch their killer. If he turned up at her bedside now, she'd be disappointed. He knew he would be, in her place. His duty was suddenly crystal clear.

Outside, the very air seemed charged with anticipation. The late afternoon light cast long shadows from the buildings around him so that he was walking in strobes of light and darkness. *Not long now.*

From somewhere far off the sound of an ambulance siren blared out. Ava? The memory of his sister Maggie lying bleeding from the neck, flashed into his mind. Then he turned the key in the ignition and drove out. To his right lay the road to the hospital. Neal checked for oncoming traffic and yanked the wheel sharp left.

Chapter Twenty-seven

Jess held back. The urge to obtain justice for Leanne nearly made her act, but she was afraid, not only for her own safety, but of crossing that line. If she rushed forward now, and plunged the knife into this man's back, it wouldn't be self-defence. It would be cold-blooded murder. She lowered her arm and watched him move hesitantly forward. He too was afraid. The air in the room was heavy with the scent of their mingled fear.

I'm so sorry for letting you down again, Leanne. For a moment Jess was back in that corridor with the girls poking fun at her and Leanne fearlessly coming to her rescue. Then she was on Stromford High Street, the first time she'd betrayed Leanne's kindness. Wind forward to Leanne being led away by the police, defiant, giving Jess a look of boundless sadness.

A pent-up sob escaped from Jess's lips. She might as well have screamed. The man spun round. Jess raised the knife. His eyes moved in confusion from her face to the knife.

He held up a hand. "Whoa."

"Stay away from me," Jess shouted.

"You've got the wrong person," he said.

"Shut up!"

"You're not police, are you? What are you doing here? Did he bring you here?" He seemed as confused as she was.

Before Jess could reply, they were both distracted by the sound of a car approaching. The man took his advantage. He strode over to Jess and knocked the knife from her hand. She froze. Without the weapon she was helpless.

But the man made no move to hurt or restrain her. He picked up the knife and then just stood there. It took a couple of moments for the penny to drop. Someone the man feared was in that car. The one who'd bound and gagged her and left her in the half darkness. Jess sidled up a bit and he moved to stand beside her. Their eyes met momentarily and he gave a slight nod.

The boat tipped and someone stepped on board.

"Seth?"

Jess suppressed a gasp. She knew that voice.

"Jonty!" she cried.

The man beside her cursed and grabbed her wrist.

"Ouch! Let go." To her surprise, Seth released his grip.

It took a moment more for Jess to understand what was happening. She looked into Jonty's eyes and saw a cold, inhuman stare. He had become someone else.

Jonty snorted. "Seriously, Seth?" His eyes went to the knife jerking nervously in Seth's hand.

"Let her go," Seth said.

"I don't think so, mate." Jonty laughed. It had no humour in it. "What are you even doing here, Seth?"

"Henry told me you'd taken his boat. I knew you'd bring it here. This is where you brought Leanne and Ruby, isn't it?"

We're two to one, Jess thought. But Jonty was huge. She'd never noticed it before. He was stooped, as always, but only because he was too tall to stand upright beneath the low ceiling of the narrowboat. How wrong she'd been! Barney hadn't been Jonty's shield, he'd been his smokescreen.

Seth took a step forward, placing himself in front of Jess. Jonty laughed again. "Quite the little gent, aren't we, Seth? Don't be fooled by this display of gallantry, Jess. Your hero's nothing more than a pathetic, filthy paedo. Tell her, Seth."

Seth was silent.

Jess guessed he was weighing up his chances. He had a weapon. Jonty was unarmed, or appeared to be. Jess froze.

Seth launched himself at Jonty, crying out to Jess, "Run! Get out of here! He'll kill you! Go!"

The two men collided with a crash. Caught behind them in the narrow space, unable to move forward, Jess was forced to witness Jonty's savage assault. He struck out in all directions, fast and hard. His first kick knocked the knife from Seth's hand. His second drove into his chest, cracking ribs and sending Seth reeling back against the partition. Jonty spun around and delivered a final kick, sending Seth to the floor with a bone-crunching crash.

It's over, Jess thought. But Jonty wasn't finished. He drove his fists into Seth's face, punching over and over until it was reduced to a pulpy mess. Jess watched in mounting horror. Would he ever stop? On and on Jonty thrashed. Even when Seth was still and quiet, the beating continued. It was sickening.

Jess saw her chance.

The knife was still lying where it had fallen from Seth's hand. With her eyes on Jonty, Jess slowly reached down and picked it up. This time there was no hesitation. She raised the knife.

"Stop!"

Barney stood in the doorway, a look of sheer horror on his face.

Jess froze. Jonty staggered to his feet, his mouth twisted in a bloody smile.

"Hey, big guy. Don't be scared. We're just having a bit of fun." He looked down. "It's not real, you know. We're acting. Just like in a movie."

Barney stared down at Seth's bloodied, lifeless form.

"What are you doing here, Barney? You were supposed to wait in the car. I told you to wait in the car."

Barney gulped. Tears began rolling down his cheeks.

"Shit!" Jonty said, "Shit." He wiped Seth's blood from his face with the back of his hand and stood, shaking his head. "Shit, Barney."

Jess recovered first. She side-stepped Seth's prone body and stumbled to the door. Looking Jonty in the eye, she laid a hand gently on Barney's arm, ready to steer him up the three wooden steps to the deck. Jonty's gaze slid from Jess's face to Barney's and he gave his brother a nod.

"Jonty." Barney said plaintively. He took a step towards Jonty. Jess tugged on his sleeve.

"Come on, Barney. Come with me now."

Together, they stumbled up the steps to the deck.

* * *

Any misgivings Neal had about going after Jonty soon dissipated. He approached the stretch of gravelled road leading to the towpath where he hoped to find the Hermione moored. Jonty had taken a risk, mooring here, but after his interview, he must have realised that it was only a matter of time before the police determined who had really murdered Leanne Jackson and Ruby Kennedy. He needed to be near enough to town to collect his brother, but far enough away to avoid immediate detection.

He had chosen an isolated stretch of the River Strom that was shrouded in woodland. Ava had provided the clue with the words 'Haunted tower.' She was alluding to a derelict World War Two RAF aviation tower that was reputedly haunted.

Neal turned a blind corner and his car screeched to a halt, inches from two running figures directly in his path. A woman, blood-spattered and apparently exhausted, slumped over the bonnet of his car, while beside her, a young man stroked her hair, muttering, 'There, there.'

Neal looked over the steering wheel and met the terrified gaze of Jess Stokes.

Neal stepped out of the car. "Police."

Jess's face crumpled with relief. "Jonty . . . he . . . he killed someone. R . . . right in front of us. He . . . just kept on . . . and on. There was so . . . much blood."

"It's alright. You're both safe now." Neal glanced around. "Where is he now?"

"On . . . on the boat," Jess said. She pointed behind her, but the river was round a curve in the road, out of sight.

Neal handed Jess the keys. "Get in the car. Lock the doors. If you see Jonty, drive off. Can you do that?"

"W. . . what about you?" Jess asked.

"Just let me do my job." Neal managed a thin smile. "Backup's on its way."

He waited until they were both in the car, then set off on foot, round the curve, and keeping close to the treeline.

The boat was dark grey, nondescript, a less colourful version of the kind of vessel people hired to drift along the county's picturesque waterways.

Two cars were parked alongside the towpath. Seth's and Jonty's? From what Jess said, Seth was already dead. Was Jonty still on the boat? Neal looked along the towpath in both directions and saw no one. It was possible that Jonty had escaped into the cover of the trees and was already on the run.

The boat had two entry points. With an eye on the bow, Neal stepped aboard at the stern and crouched to pass through some wooden doors into what seemed to be a kitchen and living area. He saw Jonty immediately. He was standing over the bloodied remains of Seth Conway. He didn't seem to have heard Neal arrive.

"Jonty Cole." Neal was about to issue the standard caution, when Jonty, suddenly animated, moved behind a partition and hid himself from sight. Neal took a couple of steps forward. "We can do this the easy way, son. Or—"

Before he could finish, there was a tearing sound and the partition came crashing down on top of him. Neal raised his hands in front of his face to shield it from the splinters of wood flying up from the demolished wall. Blood trickled down his wrists from the cuts made by shards of split pine embedded in the soft flesh of his hands and fingers.

"Or what, dickhead?"

Neal looked into Jonty's eyes. This was a man capable of ripping his victims apart, pounding them into a pulpy mess with his bare fists. As always in moments of extreme danger, thoughts of Archie rose in his mind. He blinked away the image of his son's face. Not now. There wasn't time.

Jonty bared his teeth. His face, still dripping with Seth's blood, was frozen in an expression of utter savagery. Neal had an impression of a supernatural being.

A snarl of rage erupted from deep in Jonty's throat and he flung himself at Neal, knocking him to the floor amidst the fallen timber. Before Neal could recover, Jonty straddled him and forced a broken plank against his throat, pressing down until Neal sputtered and choked.

Jonty grinned evilly. "Or what, shithead?"

Neal grasped Jonty's wrists, straining to keep some of the weight off his neck. The wood chafed against his throat, scoring the fine skin until blood began to pool against the splintered wedge of wood.

Time slowed. Neal fought to use his legs against his assailant, but his limbs seemed only to scrabble ineffectually beneath Jonty's weight. Sounds became muffled. His vision blurred. It tunnelled to a pinpoint and began to fade.

* * *

Neal didn't immediately register the release of the pressure on his windpipe, or that his vision was clearing. He was drifting slowly, willingly, towards a searing white light in the far distance.

"Jim! Breathe, you sonofabitch!" Neal felt a sudden, sharp sting on his cheek. He gasped. He breathed in, spluttered and gagged. The pressure against his throat was gone.

"Easy, sir." He blinked. It couldn't be. Ava Merry was hovering above him, her eyes full of concern.

"J . . . Jonty," he rasped. Ava smiled, and glanced to the side.

"Out for the count." She held up an object for him to see. Swirls of green and red coalesced into a design of ferns and roses on a traditional narrowboat flat iron.

"You're supposed to be in hospital."

"Lucky for you I'm not." She grinned. "I escaped from a burly paramedic and followed you here. Jess and Barney are okay. They're in your car."

"Ava?"

"Sir?"

Their eyes locked. Neal was reminded of the last words of a poem by the metaphysical poet, George Herbert — 'Something understood.'

He said, "Help me the devil up, will you?"

Chapter Twenty-eight

Ava stood outside the front door of Jim Neal's house, clutching a bottle of champagne. Before she could knock, the door was flung open and Archie Neal, restraining an excited dog, beckoned her inside.

Ava smiled. "This must be Lachie." She kneeled to allow the dog to lick her face. She thought suddenly of Jess Stokes and her friend, Pam, whom she had met while out running on the west common earlier in the day. They had been out exercising Boris, Henry Bolt's borzoi. Ava had stopped to say 'hello.'

"I still miss Bunty," Pam said, looking down at Boris who wagged his tail. "Some people think I'm crazy to adopt Boris after all his master did. But it's not his fault, is it?" She stroked Boris's brindled fur. Henry Bolt had confessed to poisoning Bunty simply because he feared that Boris would try to mate with her. But he hadn't mugged Pam, or slashed Jess's tyres. The former had most likely been Jonty's work, the latter a random act of vandalism.

Ava looked at Jess. "How are you doing?"

"I'm good," Jess said, sounding as if she meant it. "Can't wait for my moment in court." Jess had agreed, unreservedly, to testify against Jonty Cole when his case came to trial.

"And Mitch? I hope he's recovered from being a suspect?"

"He's good too." Jess smiled. "We're good. I've been accepted on an access course starting in September. I'm hoping to qualify as a teacher one day. I want to specialise in teaching kids with learning difficulties and disabilities."

"That's great news, Jess. Congratulations."

Another question hung in the air.

"Barney's going to be okay," Jess said before Ava asked. "Mitch and I are befriending him. He doesn't want to see Jonty. Not at the moment, anyway."

"Ava!" The sound of Maggie Neal's voice brought Ava back to the present. She planted a kiss on Ava's cheek. "It's great to see you! I'm so pleased you could come."

"Congratulations, Maggie." Ava kissed her back, warmly. "Let me see it, then." Maggie held out her hand for Ava to see the rose gold engagement ring Jock had given her just a week ago.

Ava gave a low whistle. "It's beautiful, Maggie."

"Thanks, Ava. Why don't you join Jim for a drink? Jock and I are just putting the finishing touches to the meal."

Ava hesitated. To tell the truth, she was a little nervous at being invited to dinner at the Neal household. She wasn't quite sure whether she was there as Neal's colleague or Maggie's friend, or both.

Maggie showed her into the living room. Neal was sitting in an armchair, reading. He looked up and gave Ava a warm smile. "Drink?" he asked, his hand already reaching towards a crystal decanter. "Whisky okay?" Ava nodded.

Maggie had disappeared and Archie had gone upstairs.

"How are you feeling?" Ava asked, looking at the necklace of fading cuts and bruises around Neal's throat. He had been hospitalised for a day and off work for a week. "Voice is nearly back to normal, I hear."

"I'm fine," Neal answered, predictably. "Ridiculous for them to insist I take so long off work. How are you?"

Ava touched the spot on her head that had collided with the sharp edge of Barney's table. Jonty had struck her with enough force to knock her off her feet. "I'm fine too. I was only out for a couple of minutes. Don't know why they insisted on me spending the night in hospital. Concussion my ar—, er, foot."

Ava took a sip of her whisky and her thoughts returned to the events of that day. She recalled finding Neal pinned to the floor, his face an unnatural shade of blue, with Jonty straddling him. She had cast about the room, looking for a weapon. The iron, with its colourful design had caught her eye. It had very nearly become a murder weapon like its counterpart. Ava hadn't cared how hard she hit Jonty. All she could think of was the colour of Neal's face and that if she didn't act fast, it would be too late.

"What's the news?" Neal asked. Ava knew what he meant and gave him an update.

"We know the whole sorry story now. We were mostly right. Leanne started fishing after she discovered that Chantelle and Michaela had died in unnatural circumstances." Ava took another sip. "Tom's liaised with the SIO who dealt with Michaela's drowning. The witness was traced and it seems that it was a genuine accident. Michaela got out of her depth. She was a poor swimmer and should never have attempted the rescue in the first place. Of course, we'll never know what was going through Michaela's mind when she jumped into the river after that dog.."

Neal gave a nod. "And Chantelle?"

Ava shrugged. "There were no witnesses. A friend's come forward this week claiming Chantelle told her she was unable to come to terms with certain 'events in her life.' She sounded suicidal, said the friend." Ava sighed. "I believe she took her own life."

They sat in silence for a moment.

Ava continued. "PJ finally tracked down Corinna Masters. Turns out she's a survivor. She changed her name to make a clean break from her past. She now works in a women's refuge in Sheffield."

They both smiled. Ava's faded first. "Jonty admits to beating both Leanne and Ruby but denies that he killed them. Liz Marlborough's going for a charge of manslaughter." Neal flinched but said nothing. There had been water in Leanne's lungs when she entered the River Strom that night. It had been an act of courage on her part to throw herself into the water, knowing that she would never make it to the bank. Her prints were all over the flat iron, as were Jonty's. She had taken it with her in a desperate bid to leave a clue behind. Ava fervently hoped it hadn't helped Jonty get off the murder charge.

"He'll be charged with Seth's murder, if that's any consolation. Jess was a witness." They reflected on that for a moment or two. Ava told Neal about their encounter on the common, and Jess's willingness to testify. Neal nodded solemnly.

"PJ and Tom have just about recovered from being sent on a wild goose chase after Seth Conway and missing all the action." Neal smiled.

Maggie came and called them to dinner.

Ava followed Neal and Archie into the dining room, which had been festooned with bunting for the occasion. She saw her bottle of champagne cooling in an ice bucket in the centre of the table. Neal lifted it out, popped the cork and filled their glasses one by one. Ava's nervousness gradually began to dissipate.

Neal raised his glass. "To my beautiful sister, Maggie. And to my best friend, Jock Dodds."

They all drank. Then Maggie stood, looking radiant. She took in the faces of everyone around the table, and made a second toast.

"To family."

THE END

Thank you for reading this book. If you enjoyed it please leave feedback on Amazon, and if there is anything we missed or you have a question about then please get in touch. The author and publishing team appreciate your feedback and time reading this book.

Our email is office@joffebooks.com

www.joffebooks.com

ALSO BY JANICE FROST

DEAD SECRET
DARK SECRET
HER HUSBAND'S SECRET
THEIR FATAL SECRETS

Printed in Poland
by Amazon Fulfillment
Poland Sp. z o.o., Wrocław